MW01109416

DISCARD

Will Hobbs

WHO
WROTE
THAT?

Will Hobbs

Hal Marcovitz

Foreword by
Kyle Zimmer

CHELSEA HOUSE PUBLISHERS
A Haights Cross Communications ✦ Company ®
Philadelphia

CHELSEA HOUSE PUBLISHERS

VP, NEW PRODUCT DEVELOPMENT Sally Cheney
DIRECTOR OF PRODUCTION Kim Shinners
CREATIVE MANAGER Takeshi Takahashi
MANUFACTURING MANAGER Diann Grasse

STAFF FOR WILL HOBBS

EXECUTIVE EDITOR Matt Uhler
EDITORIAL ASSISTANT Sarah Sharpless
PRODUCTION EDITOR Noelle Nardone
PHOTO EDITOR Sarah Bloom
INTERIOR AND COVER DESIGNER Keith Trego
LAYOUT 21st Century Publishing and Communications, Inc.

http://www.chelseahouse.com

A Haights Cross Communications ✦ Company ®

First Printing

1 3 5 7 9 8 6 4 2

Library of Congress Cataloging-in-Publication Data

Marcovitz, Hal.
   Will Hobbs/Hal Marcovitz.
      p. cm.—(Who wrote that?)
   Includes bibliographical references and index.
   ISBN 0-7910-8657-7
   1. Hobbs, Will—Juvenile literature. 2. Authors, American—20th century—
Biography—Juvenile literature. 3. Children's stories—Authorship—Juvenile
literature. 4. Wilderness areas in literature—Juvenile literature. I. Title. II. Series.
PS3558.O23Z77 2005
813'.54—dc22

                                                            2005008181

All links and Web addresses were checked and verified to be correct at the time
of publication. Because of the dynamic nature of the Web, some addresses
and links may have changed since publication and may no longer be valid.

Table of Contents

FOREWORD BY
KYLE ZIMMER
PRESIDENT, FIRST BOOK

HUMANITY IS POWERED by stories. From our earliest days as thinking beings, we employed every available tool to tell each other stories. We danced, drew pictures on the walls of our caves, spoke, and sang. All of this extraordinary effort was designed to entertain, recount the news of the day, explain natural occurrences — and then gradually to build religious and cultural traditions and establish the common bonds and continuity that eventually formed civilizations. Stories are the most powerful force in the universe; they are the primary element that has distinguished our evolutionary path.

Our love of the story has not diminished with time. Enormous segments of societies are devoted to the art of storytelling. Book sales in the United States alone topped $26 billion last year; movie studios spend fortunes to create and promote stories; and the news industry is more pervasive in its presence than ever before.

There is no mystery to our fascination. Great stories are magic. They can introduce us to new cultures, or remind us of the nobility and failures of our own, inspire us to greatness or scare us to death; but above all, stories provide human insight on a level that is unavailable through any other source. In fact, stories connect each of us to the rest of humanity not just in our own time, but also throughout history.

This special magic of books is the greatest treasure that we can hand down from generation to generation. In fact, that spark in a child that comes from books became the motivation for the creation of my organization, First Book, a national literacy program with a simple mission: to provide new books to the most disadvantaged children. At present, First Book has been at work in hundreds of communities for over a decade. Every year children in need receive millions of books through our organization and millions more are provided through dedicated literacy institutions across the United States and around the world. In addition, groups of people dedicate themselves tirelessly to working with children to share reading and stories in every imaginable setting from schools to the streets. Of course, this Herculean effort serves many important goals. Literacy translates to productivity and employability in life and many other valid and even essential elements. But at the heart of this movement are people who love stories, love to read, and want desperately to ensure that no one misses the wonderful possibilities that reading provides.

When thinking about the importance of books, there is an overwhelming urge to cite the literary devotion of great minds. Some have written of the magnitude of the importance of literature. Amy Lowell, an American poet, captured the concept when she said, "Books are more than books. They are the life, the very heart and core of ages past, the reason why men lived and worked and died, the essence and quintessence of their lives." Others have spoken of their personal obsession with books, as in Thomas Jefferson's simple statement, "I live for books." But more compelling, perhaps, is the almost instinctive excitement in children for books and stories.

Throughout my years at First Book, I have heard truly extraordinary stories about the power of books in the lives of children. In one case, a homeless child, who had been bounced from one location to another, later resurfaced—and the only possession that he had fought to keep was the book he was given as part of a First Book distribution months earlier. More recently, I met a child who, upon receiving the book he wanted, flashed a big smile and said, "This is my big chance!" These snapshots reveal the true power of books and stories to give hope and change lives.

As these children grow up and continue to develop their love of reading, they will owe a profound debt to those volunteers who reached out to them—a debt that they may repay by reaching out to spark the next generation of readers. But there is a greater debt owed by all of us—a debt to the storytellers, the authors, who have bound us together, inspired our leaders, fueled our civilizations, and helped us put our children to sleep with their heads full of images and ideas.

WHO WROTE THAT? is a series of books dedicated to introducing us to a few of these incredible individuals. While we have almost always honored stories, we have not uniformly honored storytellers. In fact, some of the most important authors have toiled in complete obscurity throughout their lives or have been openly persecuted for the uncomfortable truths that they have laid before us. When confronted with the magnitude of their written work or perhaps the daily grind of our own, we can forget that writers are people. They struggle through the same daily indignities and dental appointments, and they experience the intense joy and bottomless despair that many of us do. Yet somehow they rise above it all to deliver a powerful thread that connects us all. It is a rare honor to have the opportunity that these books provide to share the lives of these extraordinary people. Enjoy.

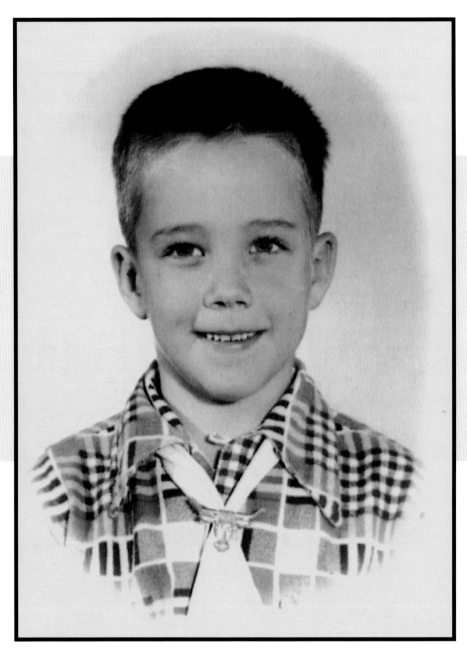

In his 1988 novel Changes in Latitudes, *Will Hobbs tells the story of two young Americans trying to save endangered sea turtles in Mexico. The characters are based partly on Hobbs himself, who as a young boy in Falls Church, Virginia, was fascinated with the local box turtles.*

1

Plight of the Sea Turtles

SEA TURTLES ARE now recovering off the coast of Mexico. In the late 1980s they had been driven to the brink of extinction. For decades, hunters had captured and killed the large aquatic reptiles. Indeed, it seemed as though there was no part of the turtle that couldn't be sold for profit. The skin could be tanned into leather and sold to manufacturers of shoes, belts, wallets, and ladies' handbags. The meat could be cooked and eaten. The very soft and jelly-like portion found along the inside of the shell known as the "calipee" was used to make turtle soup.

Author Will Hobbs wrote about the dangers faced by olive ridley turtles—small, hard-shelled marine turtles named for their olive-green-colored shell—in his 1988 novel *Changes in Latitudes*. The story is based in Mexico and follows two young Americans, Travis and Teddy, as they discover the abuse of olive ridley turtles. During the story, they find themselves caught up in environmentalist efforts to save the reptiles. The two brothers meet a marine biologist named Casey, who explains what is happening to the turtles on a beach near where their family is vacationing.

Hobbs based the character of Teddy partly on himself. In the book, it is Teddy, the younger of the two brothers, who feels strongest about saving the turtles. The story even tells how a 4-year-old boy, Teddy, led a rescue mission to save box turtles in his neighborhood. "Kids would paw them all day, and turn them on their backs over and over again just to see them right themselves," Travis explains in the book. "Teddy got to where he wasn't thinking about anything else but those poor box turtles living in captivity."[1]

That story is based on an event in Hobbs's life when the author lived as a young boy in Falls Church, Virginia. Hobbs recalls:

> Falls Church is where I started school, and where I should have saved the baseball cards we pinned to the spokes of our bikes. The fluttering sound of those Willie Mays, Mickey Mantle, and Joe DiMaggio cards is still vivid, and so is the feel of a box turtle in my hand. How I loved those box turtles. Their shape, their markings, their eyes, their claws, the scales on their feet, their ability to close up tight, to flip themselves over—well, I admired everything about them. Only bears, later on, came to rival turtles as my totems.

Did you know...

Will Hobbs once helped to save sea turtles. While camping on a remote beach along the Pacific coast of Mexico, Hobbs and his wife Jean spent five days working with a group of Mexican biologists and their students to protect the eggs of leatherback turtles from poachers.

At night, the female leatherbacks would emerge from the sea and crawl onto the beach to lay their eggs. The Hobbses and the students would collect the eggs before the females covered them, and then bury them in a protected nursery. After 60 days, the eggs would hatch into baby leatherbacks.

"At the time we were there, there were lots of hatchlings clawing their way to the surface from the earlier 'plantings,'" says Hobbs. "It was a big thrill to take them outside the fence and watch them disappear into the sea. In my novel, Travis said they look like wind-up toys. They really do."*

Sea turtles are now protected by the Mexican and U.S. governments. Still, thousands are killed accidentally when they are caught in nets cast by commercial shrimp boats. The turtles become tired and drown when caught in the nets. To prevent sea turtles from getting caught in nets, commercial fishermen are urged to use a "Turtle Excluder Device." The apparatus is a ring of steel bars that fits over the mouth of a shrimp net. When turtles or other large sea creatures, such as sharks, strike the ring of bars, they are ejected instead of drawn into the net.

* "Will Hobbs Talks about *Changes in Latitude*," *Will Hobbs Official Website*—Changes in Latitudes *Idea Page*, www.willhobbsauthor.com/ bookspages/book%20ideas%20pages/changeslatit.html.

The woods behind our house was an incredible box-turtle habitat. Turtle hunters of our prowess and dedication had little trouble finding them. We could keep them only three days; such was the rule my big brothers laid down. By the fourth day, we returned them to the spot where we had found them. It was a whole lot like catch-and-release fishing. One time Greg and Ed became aware that some neighbor kids had a couple dozen box turtles in their backyard. They kept them on a permanent basis. Somehow I don't recall us trying to talk them out of this practice. When no one was at home, we nabbed every one of their turtles, liberated them into the woods, and forever kept our mouths shut. It's an incident fraught with moral ambiguity, but one that had an epic quality to a five-year-old.[2]

Changes in Latitudes was Hobbs's first published book. Hobbs says that initially he came up with the idea for the story when he saw a photograph of a sea turtle in a *National Geographic* magazine. He found himself struck by the beauty of the creature. Hobbs says he wrote a short story about sea turtles, telling what it must be like to swim alongside one of the graceful reptiles. His character Travis describes the experience in *Changes in Latitudes*: "For the first time in my life I was filled with awe. I was overwhelmed with the kind of appreciation for them that Teddy must have felt. As beautiful and perfect as wild geese, they swam like birds of the sea. Just as birds had mastered flight, these turtles were reptiles who'd taken to the open sea. If anything, they were more graceful than birds because the water slowed their movement to the speed of a hypnotic dance."[3]

Later, Hobbs decided to write a novel-length story about the dangers faced by sea turtles. He got the idea when he visited the Yucatan peninsula in Mexico. At the time, he was on vacation.

> I came across a sea turtle in a three-sided pen at the beach, and encountered many sea turtle products for sale. Back home I read an exposé of an outfit on the Pacific coast of Mexico that was slaughtering tens of thousands of ridley sea turtles every year while merely pretending to hatch their eggs. All of these things started to come together. I started imagining a novel that would intertwine the fates of endangered turtles with that of an 'endangered family' on spring break in Mexico.[4]

Changes in Latitudes is, in fact, about a lot more than just saving olive ridley sea turtles. For starters, the title is based on a song by the singer Jimmy Buffet called "Changes in Latitudes, Changes in Attitudes." According to Hobbs, the song title fit the story in the book perfectly. In the book, the main character, Travis, is a selfish and self-centered teenager. The book shows how Travis learns to appreciate the needs of others while his family spends a vacation in Mexico. Hobbs says, "Travis's changes in attitudes is what this story is all about. Over the course of the novel, he moves from being self-absorbed to caring a whole lot more about his family and even about the endangered sea turtles that his little brother loves so much."[5]

And, as Hobbs explains, Travis's family is "endangered." The children's parents are thinking about getting a divorce. Their mother has taken them to Mexico to try to sort things out. Travis attempts to hide from his problems and his parents' approaching breakup by escaping into his own "cool" world. Travis and Teddy's sister Jennifer becomes more and more anxious as she carries the weight of her family's troubles on her own shoulders. Teddy becomes

The ability to play and use the imagination is important for the developing writer, even at a very young age. When Will Hobbs was young, he enjoyed playing baseball, fishing, hiking, and collecting snakes and lizards. Here a young Hobbs (left) plays "Wild West" with his brothers, Ed and Greg.

obsessed with the sea turtles and dies while trying to rescue a turtle. The boy suffers an aneurysm, which is a burst artery in the brain. Only after Teddy's death does Travis realize he can't hide from his problems and decides to carry on Teddy's crusade to save the turtles. On the family's final night in Mexico, Travis returns to the turtle pens where Teddy died. "All night I freed turtles," Travis says in the book. "My heart was big enough and my back strong enough to carry the load. One by one I carried them in Teddy's footsteps around the poles to the sea. The sun was rising as the last one trudged forward, gained deep water, and disappeared."[6]

Writing in *Horn Book*, a magazine that reports on young people's literature, reviewer Nancy Vasilakis talked about *Changes in Latitudes*. She said the book "neatly balances the perilous situation of these ancient lumbering sea creatures against the breakdown of [a] family." She said Hobbs showed a "sensitive ear for the language of the young."[7]

Since *Changes in Latitudes* was published, Hobbs has written 14 more novels. He has also written two picture books for beginning readers. Each book serves as a vehicle for Hobbs to show his devotion to the environment. In his books, Hobbs writes about the plight of birds, sea creatures, and mammals whose homes are threatened and abused by people. As for olive ridley sea turtles, the animals are now protected. In 1990, Mexico's government adopted a law prohibiting capture of the reptiles for any purpose. The eggs have received special protection. People caught selling sea turtle eggs face prison terms.

Hobbs says, "You know, the idea of swimming with sea turtles is all that survived from my original short story. But it was plenty. I wrapped the whole novel around that image. It taught me that an image you have a strong feeling about is all that you need to get started. Starting with a single image, you could write a poem, a short story, or an entire novel."[8]

Will Hobbs's father was an officer in the U.S. Air Force, so the family moved frequently during his childhood. He lived in Panama, Alaska, Texas, and California. The frequent moves instilled in Hobbs a love for adventure that is reflected in all of his books. This family photo was taken in Panama.

2

Chasing His Secret Dream

WHEN HOBBS WAS a young boy attending Mount Spurr Elementary School in Alaska, his teacher read the book *Call It Courage* out loud to the class. Written in 1940 by English author Armstrong Sperry, *Call It Courage* tells the story of Mafatu, a young Polynesian boy who overcomes his fear of the sea to become a brave chief. The story follows Mafatu as he lives through a storm at sea and finds himself lost on a deserted island. But Mafatu overcomes his fears. He kills a shark and a wild boar, evades cannibals, and makes his escape in a dugout canoe.

For young Hobbs, the story opened his eyes to the world of literature. The experience prompted him to start thinking about the many exotic places on Earth where adventure might await the reader. "On my way to school during those weeks, I was in a sort of trance," he says. "No matter that it was dark and the middle of the winter in Alaska, I was in the South Seas, in an outrigger canoe. After fourth grade I was on automatic when it came to reading."[9]

Hobbs is the son of a U.S. Air Force officer. As a typical military family of the era, the Hobbses moved many times from base to base whenever Will's father was transferred. Most U.S. Air Force bases have been established in remote locations so the noise of heavy jet aircraft engines does not disturb local residents. As such, the families of the Air Force servicemen often find themselves living adjacent to undeveloped land. Indeed, Hobbs grew up on the edge of wilderness in Alaska, California, and Texas.

William Carl Hobbs was born in Pittsburgh, Pennsylvania, on August 22, 1947, the son of Gregory and Mary Hobbs. Hobbs remembers the city of his birth from many visits to his grandparents over the years, but before he was a year old the family left for the Panama Canal Zone. That is where his father, an engineer, had been assigned to duty. At the time, Will was the youngest of three Hobbs boys. A sister, Barbara, and another brother, Joe, would follow later. Hobbs has few memories of Panama, but does recall the wildlife of the Central American country. He remembers when a sun bear, also known as a honey bear, chased the Hobbs family during an outing.

When Hobbs was 4 years old, the family returned to the United States. They settled in Falls Church, Virginia. At the time, Gregory Hobbs had been assigned to duty at the Pentagon, the headquarters of the American armed forces in Washington, D.C. It was in Falls Church where Hobbs started elementary school, collected baseball cards, and developed a love for box turtles.

The Hobbses did not stay in Virginia for long. Will began third grade as a student in Anchorage, Alaska, where his father had been assigned to Elmendorf Air Force Base. The beauty of the Alaskan landscape made a permanent impression on Hobbs. "Alaska is where I imprinted on big mountains, big rivers, glaciers, salmon runs, moose and bears, the northern lights, the winter darkness and the midnight sun. My novels *Far North, Jason's Gold*, and *Down the Yukon* hearken back to strong impressions and emotions from my Alaska years," he says.[10]

The Hobbs family spent several years in Alaska. At first, the family lived in Anchorage. At the time, the mid-1950s, the city was much smaller than it is today. Gregory and Mary Hobbs found the house in Anchorage uncomfortable. It was cold and drafty on winter mornings. For the second year of Gregory's duty at Elmendorf, the Hobbs family found a more comfortable house on the base. For the active and playful Hobbs boys—Greg, Ed and Will—the move to Elmendorf satisfied their need for more space and more places to have fun and find mischief. Hobbs says "There was a great toboggan and saucer run" on the base. He recalls:

When we crashed, it didn't hurt. We were bundled up like astronauts. We learned to ski, after a fashion, on the base ski hill, bombing from top to bottom. The back of our quarters opened up on the parade grounds and big views of the Chugach Mountains, snow-covered all summer long. Mostly, we hung out at the baseball field. The summer days were endless, and sometimes we actually played baseball at midnight, just to say we did. I was a pitcher in the Pee Wee League . . . These were my glory days. I peaked early.[11]

Hobbs learned to fish in Alaska. During the summer, Gregory Hobbs would take his sons to the Kenai River,

Did you know...

Will Hobbs may have inherited his love for the wilderness from his great-grandfather, Will Rhodes, for whom he is named. Rhodes was the marshal of Dodge City, Kansas, for 10 years starting in 1892. Dodge City earned its wild reputation from the many cattle rustlers, cowboys, and gunslingers who passed through town. Dodge City was also the home, for a time, of the legendary Marshal Wyatt Earp.

By the time Will Rhodes was named marshal, Dodge City's days as a gunslingers' town were over. When Rhodes took over as marshal, the gunfighters had all been long dead and buried. In fact, most of them were buried at a place known as "Boot Hill." It was Rhodes who came up with the idea of making Boot Hill a tourist attraction. He put up colorful grave markers for the outlaws and invited tourists to come out and see them. Rhodes's interest in making Boot Hill a tourist attraction earned him the nickname "Boot Hill Bill." Today, tourists can find a museum at Boot Hill that provides a history of Dodge City's role in the days of the old West.

where they fished for salmon and trout. "It's not that I caught many fish there," Hobbs recalls:

> What will never fade is the sound of the river and the motion of the current, seeing those monstrous bear tracks in the mud, watching my dad in his hip waders fish deeper water than I could reach, witnessing a king salmon make short work of Greg's tackle. No sooner had Greg hooked the chinook salmon than it made a run for the current. His reel more or less exploded.[12]

Back home, Gregory Hobbs maintained a vegetable garden. He taught Hobbs how to till the soil and make things grow. At school, Hobbs was a good student. He worked hard, although he admits that his chief reason for achieving high grades was his grandfather's promise of 50 cents for every A on his report card.

The Hobbs family's stay in Alaska came to an end in November 1957. Gregory Hobbs was transferred to an assignment in northern California. Hobbs recalled there were "tears streaming down my face" as the family stood on the deck of a Navy ship heading south from Kodiak Island.[13] The family settled in Marin County, California. Today, Marin County is a busy suburb of San Francisco with a population of 250,000 people. In the 1950s, however, Marin County had more of a rural quality. It featured hills covered with wild oat grass, bay trees, and buckeye chestnut trees. The Hobbses settled in Terra Linda, a community of 2,000 people, located about 20 miles north of San Francisco. Hobbs says: "Terra Linda was a kids' paradise, and . . . there was no shortage of kids to enjoy it with. Our house wasn't big by today's standards, but it had two bathrooms, which was the height of luxury, and a family room over the garage. It was on a hillside that was mostly rock when we moved in."[14]

As in Alaska, the Hobbs family planted a vegetable garden alongside the house. Hobbs grew his own tomatoes, cucumbers, melons, and pumpkins. After school, Hobbs and his brothers would slide down Marin County's grassy hills. They cut up cardboard boxes into sheets that served as sleds. The Hobbs boys were big baseball fans. They attended the home games of the San Francisco Giants, a baseball team that had just moved to California from New York City. Hobbs was an excellent pitcher himself. He once struck out the side on only nine pitches during a Little League game. Meanwhile, on his own, Hobbs wandered through the nearby hills. He searched for snakes and lizards, which he brought to school and showed off in a terrarium his sixth-grade teacher kept in the classroom. He says:

> Reptiles came first, but any sort of critter fascinated me, even skunks . . . When my cousin Carl was visiting once from Indianapolis, we wanted to see what would happen if we cornered one. We found a perfect opportunity, right against the water tower. Somehow we were surprised when that skunk turned around and let us have it. We ran home in a state of high reek. My mother thought we were amusing.[15]

At school, Hobbs was a dedicated reader. He was a fixture in the library at Bernard Hoffman Elementary School in Terra Linda. He liked mysteries, science fiction novels, and adventure stories. He also read a lot of nonfiction, including many biographies. Among his favorite books were *Treasure Island* by Robert Louis Stevenson, *Tom Sawyer* by Mark Twain, and everything written by Jules Verne, the French science fiction author. He also read the adventure stories featuring the Hardy Boys and Tom Swift.

Hobbs joined the Boy Scouts. The organization would help him further develop his fascination for nature, his love

The setting for Will Hobbs's novels Bearstone *and* Beardance *is "the Window," a stunning rock formation along the continental divide in southwest Colorado. Hobbs lives in nearby Durango and has hiked through this area many times.*

for the outdoors, and his appreciation for the beauty of the wilderness. As a Boy Scout, Hobbs hiked through northern California's Sierra Mountains. He also explored mines left over from the Gold Rush days. In the eighth grade, Hobbs made Eagle Scout.

After spending a few months in San Bernardino in southern California, the Hobbs family was on the move again. They moved to a home on the grounds of Randolph Air Force Base, 18 miles from San Antonio. Now starting the ninth grade, Hobbs enrolled in Central Catholic High School in San Antonio. At Central Catholic, he discovered that all the students were expected to participate in the U.S. Army's Reserve Officer Training Program, known as ROTC. "Twice a week we wore our ROTC uniforms to school,"

Hobbs says. "We drilled with M-1 rifles on the macadam behind the school. We were expected to keep our uniforms pressed and starched, our boots and brass polished to a high shine."[16] Meanwhile, Hobbs became active in student life at Central Catholic. He joined the student newspaper as well as the speech and debate clubs. At the end of his junior year, Hobbs was elected student body president.

The work at Central Catholic was difficult, but Hobbs found himself devoted to his studies. He enjoyed the challenge of maintaining high grades. It was at Central Catholic that Hobbs started developing his craft as a writer. He let himself be guided by two English teachers, Maurice Enderle and Brother Martin McMurtrey. "They had a whole lot to do with me starting to think that one day maybe I would become a writer," Hobbs says. "Both of them had extremely high standards, and Brother Mac was a published writer of short stories . . . . Both understood the value of reading. They would raise your grade one percentage point for every extra book report you made. I did a ton of reading at Central."[17]

He was still an active Boy Scout. In 1962, Hobbs escaped the unbearable heat of the Texas summer by camping along the Minnesota-Canadian border. He spent weeks on a canoe trip paddling over the many lakes and rivers in the region. The following summer, Hobbs spent a month camping at the Philmont Scout Ranch, which covers more than 215 square miles of rocky and remote ground in New Mexico. "It's mostly high country, and the air was cool, nothing at all like south Texas. After a fifteen-hour bus ride, it was thrilling to see those peaks on the horizon. As it has been for hundreds of thousands of kids from around the country, Philmont was my first introduction to the Rocky Mountains."[18] In later summers, Hobbs worked as a ranger, guide, and camp director at Philmont.

Hobbs left Central Catholic before graduation because his father was transferred back to Hamilton Air Force Base in Marin County. He recalls his senior year at Marin Catholic High School as a letdown. He was new and had to make new friends. Also, he had left a school where he excelled and served as a leader of many student organizations. Although he made the golf team, a sport he never played before moving back to Marin, he remained mostly an outsider. "On spring weekends I went on long rides on my ten-speed in west Marin, out to Point Reyes National Seashore and back over the shoulder of Mount Tamalpais. They were monster rides, up to eighty miles, before people thought that sort of thing was fun. It helped me battle my mind parasites."[19]

Hobbs narrowed his college search down to two schools. He had decided to go to either Stanford University near San Francisco or the University of Notre Dame in South Bend, Indiana. He chose Notre Dame, mostly because his older brother Greg had already enrolled there. Months after arriving on campus, Hobbs decided he had made a mistake. At Notre Dame, he says, there were "only guys, guys who were a lot like me, no girls at all, and not much to cheer about except big-time football."[20]

It was at Notre Dame, though, that Hobbs's talent as a writer started to flourish. An English literature professor pulled Hobbs aside one day and told him his work was very good. He told Hobbs he would do well to consider English as a major. "This was major encouragement," Hobbs says.[21]

Hobbs transferred to Stanford for his sophomore year. Following the advice of the Notre Dame professor, he declared English as his major. Hobbs read many books and fully embraced his studies. He welcomed the opportunities his classes provided to write short stories, poems, and plays. Hobbs developed an interest in anthropology. He found himself fascinated by the history and traditions of American Indians. He spent part of his junior year abroad, studying in Germany. Will Hobbs graduated with honors in 1969 and was accepted as a graduate student at Stanford. Hobbs intended to earn a doctorate in American literature and teach at the college level.

He passed his qualifying exams for the Ph.D., but concluded that he wasn't cut out to be a scholar and professor. He wanted to write fiction and to become a published author. And so he left graduate school with a master's degree and moved in with some friends in northern California. He wrote poetry and tended a vegetable garden he planted in the backyard. To make ends meet, he found a job as a fruit picker and worked briefly in a lumber mill. In fact, Hobbs would work at a number of odd jobs over the next two years. Finally, in late December 1971, Hobbs and his fiancée Jean Loftus found jobs teaching at Upper Lake Elementary School, located near Clear Lake in northern California. Hobbs says: "The pay was $17 dollars a day and for some strange reason I loved it, the work that is. I found out that I really liked working with kids, getting them excited about reading and writing."[22]

Upper Lake Elementary School had limited resources. The school could provide Hobbs with few books for his classes. Still, he encouraged his students to write and to read poetry, short stories, essays, and newspaper articles. He sent his students to the town library to find books they could read for school projects. Back in the classroom, Hobbs read aloud to his students. He used the school mimeograph machine to publish a student literary magazine. "Seeing their work in print was a huge motivation for them," he says.[23]

Hobbs became a very popular teacher at Upper Lake Elementary School. School administrators invited him back for the next year, but Hobbs declined. Jean had found a better teaching job near Santa Fe, New Mexico. They were married there on December 20, 1972. Hobbs earned his teaching certificate at nearby Highlands University in Las Vegas, New Mexico. They soon moved to Pagosa Springs, Colorado, where Hobbs was hired to teach high school English and Jean was assigned to a class at the elementary school. They also bought their first home. The Hobbses stayed in southwestern Colorado for four years. It was a fulfilling time.

Hobbs recalls that an unexpected surprise came with the teaching job in Pagosa:

> A couple of weeks after school started, I happened to discover in the student handbook that I was the director of the school plays. Staying for evening play practice was tough when you lived twenty miles out of town, especially when it was snowing, but I made the most of it. The community turned out in droves for the plays, and both the kids and I felt a tremendous sense of accomplishment when the plays came off so well. My favorite was a melodrama and a vaudeville show. After two years, though, the play practice was wearing me out. I transferred a hundred yards away and started teaching seventh grade English in the junior high.
>
> Seventh grade turned out to be a perfect fit for me. I enjoyed the energy and the enthusiasm, all those hands in the air. My principal, Terry Alley, let me start a class called "Living in the Southwest." It was a class that combined literature, social studies, and natural science, all focused on the local area. The kids interviewed local pioneers from railroading and sheepherding days. We visited the old general store at the all-but-abandoned town of Gato [Pagosa Junction] and hiked to the ancient pueblo ruins at Chimney Rock. Years later, as I was writing *Bearstone* and *Beardance*, I drew on some of what I'd learned along with the kids.[24]

Still, Hobbs ached to be a writer. The Hobbses quit their jobs and moved to Oregon. Hobbs enrolled in graduate school, intending to complete his degree and earn his doctorate in literature. After a semester, he and Jean found themselves longing for the Rocky Mountains they had left behind. The couple returned to southwestern Colorado, where they both searched for teaching jobs. This time they settled in the Durango area. Durango is located near the Four Corners area, the geographic point where the corners of four states— Utah, Arizona, New Mexico, and Colorado—meet in one place. The region is among the most picturesque in America, with mountains and mesas as tall as 14,000 feet. There are also plenty of forests, white-water rivers, blue-water lakes, and herds of grazing elk. For Hobbs, a dedicated outdoorsman, Durango would be his last stop. In 1978, he landed a job teaching seventh grade English at Miller Junior High School in Durango. It would be a job that he would hold for the next 10 years of his life. Hobbs recalls:

> As a junior high English and reading teacher, I had surrounded myself and my students with five or six hundred novels. My principal, Jules Koss, was always supportive: 'I've got a little money left over; want to order any more books?' Maybe it was the feel of those books in my hands. I couldn't stand it that I wasn't chasing my secret dream. I was a do-it-yourselfer from way back; it was time to write my own book. I would write a novel like the ones in my classroom, written especially for kids.[25]

In the summer of 1980, Hobbs wrote a manuscript titled *Pride of the West*. The gold mine in the story was inspired by an actual gold mine of the same name owned by a friend of Hobbs, an old rancher. The rancher inspired the character of the rancher in Hobbs's story. Hobbs says, "My friend, who was the starting point for the old man in the story, was always talking about reopening his mine. I thought his chances were slim in real life; why not have a go at making it happen in the story?"[26]

Hobbs centered the story at the "Window," a stunning rock formation along the continental divide in the Weminuche Wilderness of southwest Colorado. Hobbs describes the Window as "one of the sacred places in the geography of my heart."[27] While writing the book, he used details about ranching that he had learned by helping his friend bring in his hay. Finally, Hobbs decided to make the main character a Ute Indian boy, which gave him the chance to explore his interest in Native American culture.

Pride of the West would not find a publisher for eight years. In the meantime, Hobbs rewrote the story many times. After six revisions, Hobbs finally found a publisher for the book. By now, he had changed the title to *Bearstone*. It would be the first novel he wrote, but not his first published novel. (That book would turn out to be *Changes in Latitudes.*) He drew his inspiration for *Bearstone* from the vast wilderness that surrounds Durango. He also made use of his experiences hiking through the rough Rocky Mountains. When he finished the book, Hobbs fulfilled a destiny that shone on him since he was a student at Mount Spurr Elementary School in Alaska, where he listened to his teacher read *Call It Courage*. Hobbs says: "When I held that first copy of my first book in my hand, I couldn't believe it. My dream had come true."[28]

Will Hobbs and his wife, Jean, both worked as school teachers when they moved to Durango, Colorado, in the late 1970s. Many of the young characters in Hobbs's novels are at least partially based on students that they encountered in their classes. This photo is of the couple on their wedding day.

3

Caring About His Characters

CLOYD ATCITTY IS the main character in *Bearstone*, the first book written by Will Hobbs. In *Bearstone*, Hobbs uses themes that are found in many of his books. The themes include Hobbs's vivid descriptions of nature at its most beautiful as well as his decision to wrap his stories around a truly exciting adventure. Each book, to a greater or lesser degree, draws attention to the struggle of the natural world to survive. In *Bearstone*, for example, readers learn about grizzly bears, which have been driven toward near extinction. Other books center on the plight of sea turtles, condors, and even wildlife living in cities and suburbs.

Cloyd is a 14-year-old Ute Indian boy who lives in a group home for Native American youths. He doesn't try to do well in school and fails all his classes. He can barely read. His father abandoned Cloyd when he was young. His mother is dead. Cloyd was raised by his grandmother, who gave him a lot of love. She told him, "Live in a good way."[29] Still, his tribe's leaders have sent him to live in the group home because his grandmother allows him to tend her goats instead of making him go to school.

In each of Hobbs's books, his characters learn valuable lessons about nature. They also learn many lessons about *human* nature, including what is in their own hearts. Cloyd is a boy with many problems, but he has a good heart and usually means well. He is smarter than people believe him to be. He also has moral strength. But what is most easily noticed is his problem responding to authority; he doesn't often choose to do what most would consider the right thing. "For any kind of story, you need a character with a problem," says Hobbs. "For Cloyd, it's a problem with a capital 'P.'"[30]

In *Bearstone*, Susan, the head of Cloyd's group home, has arranged for Cloyd to spend the summer working on a farm owned by an older man named Walter Landis, whose wife has just died. Just before arriving at the farm, Cloyd jumps out of Susan's van and flees into the countryside. At first, Cloyd plans to hitchhike back to his grandmother's house, but while roaming nearby he finds a cave that serves as the burial chamber for an infant from the time of the cliff dwellers. Near the baby's bones, Cloyd finds a smooth stone shaped like a grizzly bear.

As he turned the pot on its side to admire it, something moved inside. He let the loose object fall gently into his hand. His heart leaped to see a small blue stone about two inches long, worn smooth by long handling. Turquoise. Two eyes, a snout, and a humped back. A bear. Surely, a bear to accompany the infant on the long journey.[31]

Finding the bearstone reminds Cloyd of what his grandmother taught him about bears and the Ute people. She taught him that bears are the most important animals of all, and that they bring strength and luck to the Ute people. Cloyd decides to keep the bearstone, believing it will give him strength "on his own life's journey."[32] And so he goes back to Walter's house, where he agrees to spend the summer working for the old man.

In later books, Hobbs sometimes wrote about young people who have hurt people or animals. Some of his characters suffer emotional trauma after seeing other people die. In *Downriver*, Hobbs wrote about seven teenagers who participate in an outdoors survival camp they call "Hoods in the Woods." All seven characters have either broken the law or are simply uncontrollable by their parents. One of the characters in *Downriver* stabbed someone. Another lived on city streets for three years. Hobbs says he decided to write about young people in trouble for several reasons. As a teacher, he had worked with many kids who had significant problems. As a writer, he finds that characters who must bear difficult problems help make the story more compelling and interesting.

In *Bearstone*, Cloyd receives this important piece of advice from Walter: "The hurt you get over makes you stronger."[33] Cloyd tries to overcome his problems on his own, but melts down in frustration and anger, all but destroying one of the few good things in his life: his relationship with Walter who actually cares about him. Cloyd tries again, and he and Walter ride into the mountains together where they form an even stronger bond.

In *Bearstone*, Hobbs also establishes the technique of basing many of his characters on real people. Walter, of course, is modeled after Hobbs's old friend who owned the real Pride of the West gold mine and who Hobbs helped over several summers. Some of the scenes in *Bearstone* are drawn directly from Hobbs's experience on the ranch. For example, Hobbs has Cloyd throw hay bales onto a trailer pulled by Walter's tractor. That is exactly the type of work Hobbs did on the ranch.

Cloyd is based on a student taught by Jean Hobbs in a Durango classroom. Hobbs says, "My wife was a teacher and she'd been telling me about a Ute boy she was working with, helping him learn to read. He was about thirteen, and had been sent from Utah to the Native American group home in Durango. She would tell me how homesick he was. My story is fiction, but her student inspired Cloyd. I'd been to the Utes' bear dance and knew how significant the kinship between people and bears was to Ute culture."[34]

Bearstone would also be the first of many books in which Hobbs centers the action in the Four Corners region. In fact, Hobbs places Walter's farm east of Durango. The characters will encounter the sights, smells, and sounds that hikers and campers encounter as they make their way through the forests, mountains, and deserts of the Four Corners area. In one important scene in *Bearstone*, Cloyd and his horse Blueboy climb a mountain known as the Rio Grande Pyramid and enter the Window, the mountain pass along the Continental Divide.

A lone giant, the Pyramid, loomed above and only a few miles away. He wondered if it could really be climbed. Close at hand, a spectacular formation in the Divide caught his fancy. It was called the Window, and it was so close he could see birds flying in the wide gap between its sheer walls. They were small birds, and they seemed to be flying loops for the sheer joy of it. They come to play, he realized. The air must pour through there like anything . . . . He noticed a bit of an elk trail leading to the Window across the steep scree slides of fine rock. On the spur of the moment, he said to the roan, "You want to stand in that Window, Blueboy? I sure do."[35]

Hobbs rarely writes about a part of the world he hasn't seen for himself. Nor does he put a character through an ordeal that he hasn't, in some way, experienced first-hand. Take, for example, a hailstorm that nearly costs Cloyd his life.

> In minutes the meadow was carpeted with a layer of hail. All of a sudden, it was winter. Cloyd had seen hailstorms in the high desert, but not like this one. Here the air itself had turned freezing cold. Shaking now from fear as well as cold, he forced himself to think. Managing another hundred yards to the trees meant nothing now. He had to reach camp, the old man, and a fire—or freeze to death.[36]

Hobbs says he was able to describe the type of hailstorm that suddenly rains down in the Four Corners area because he was once caught in a storm very much like the one that caught Cloyd. "Not only was I caught in a hailstorm like that, but a hailstorm in that exact meadow," says Hobbs. "The scenes in *Bearstone* are all places I know in my head and heart through my backpacking trips."[37] Hobbs says that when he writes, he reaches deep into his memory to recall experiences and images that he can use in a story. "These are places and situations I know so well, so it's natural to place my characters in them," he says. "When writing *Bearstone*, I thought of that hailstorm."[38]

Bearstone follows Cloyd and Walter as they head for Walter's mine in the mountains with the idea of reopening the Pride of the West and digging for gold. For Walter, the journey will mean fulfillment of a dream he's had since he gave up mining for farming 40 years ago. For Cloyd, the trip will give him the opportunity to explore the high country of the Weminuche Wilderness in the San Juan Mountains, homeland of his people, the Weminuche Utes. During the journey, Cloyd sees a grizzly bear, even though they are believed to be extinct in that part of Colorado. Cloyd commits a grave error, though, when he tells Walter about the bear in the presence of a hunter. Even though killing grizzlies is a federal crime, Cloyd suspects that the hunter intends to bag the bear for a trophy. So he follows the hunter and tries to protect the grizzly, but is unable to save the bear. While he is gone, Walter suffers a serious injury in a mining accident. When Cloyd returns, he finds the old man barely alive. Cloyd pulls Walter from the mine and saves his life.

During the ordeal, Cloyd does a lot of growing up. He takes a very large step toward manhood, experiencing the process known as "coming of age" while trying to save the bear and saving Walter. Indeed, by the time readers reach the conclusion of *Bearstone*, they realize the book is not just an adventure story. It is also a story about the love that grows between a lonely old man and a boy who never knew his own father.

Hobbs says: "That's what happens when you start writing a good story—the characters become so important. Cloyd and Walter ended up helping each other realize their dreams. I'm really pleased when students and teachers point out that the big themes in *Bearstone* are found in a saying of Cloyd's grandmother, 'Live in a good way,' and in a saying of Walter's, 'The hurt you get over makes you stronger.' That's definitely what *Bearstone* is all about."[39]

With *Bearstone*, Hobbs stakes out the turf he will tread often throughout his career as a novelist. A number of his characters will be young and troubled like Cloyd and they will also work their way through their troubles while learning about themselves and others. Hobbs's books will take his readers into some of the most beautiful parts of the North American landscape. Readers will follow his characters as

Did you know...

Will Hobbs keeps his backpack in his office, close by his desk. It is the same backpack he owned as a teenager. Hobbs says he has never found a reason to replace it.

Hobbs has backpacked more than 30 times into the Weminuche Wilderness, the rugged region of forests and mountains near his home in Durango, Colorado. "I like to go for a week at a time, visiting the high lakes and streams," he says.

> Everything I need for a week is on my back, from my tent to three meals a day. My nieces and nephews have gone on quite a few of these trips with me, and of course, Jean loves hiking in these mountains.
>
> "My backpack is like an old friend. We've been hiking together for thirty years now. We've gone a lot of places that horses could never reach. It offers me the satisfaction of cruising to amazing places on my own two feet.[*]

In addition to backpacking and rowing his raft down white water rivers, Hobbs also enjoys gardening, reading, and studying archaeology, natural history, and paleontology.

[*] "Just for Fun!" Will Hobbs Official Website, *www.willhobbsauthor.com/forfun.html*.

they climb mountains, raft down white water rivers, swim with sea turtles, fish for salmon in Alaska, and explore the wilderness of the Yukon.

Bearstone proved to be so popular among readers that Hobbs wrote a sequel titled *Beardance*, which was published in 1993. Cloyd and Walter return in the sequel, this time to find a lost Spanish gold mine. While riding through the wilderness with Walter, they are told another grizzly bear has been seen nearby. Cloyd witnesses the death of a mother grizzly and one of her cubs, and attempts to keep her two orphaned cubs alive, risking his life high in the mountains with winter closing in. Again, Hobbs describes terrain he has traveled and sights he has seen, including a massive rain of water, ice, and rocks that come sliding down a mountain. In his story, it's the same event, in the same location, that kills the mother grizzly bear.

Hobbs says that *Beardance* at first was difficult to write. He had already written a substantial part of the book when he felt he was stalling out and paused to go backpacking through the Window. He says,

> I'd already written ten or so chapters when I hiked back up to the Window, but didn't feel very good about them. They took place down on Walter's farm. Standing in the Window at 12,857 feet I could imagine I saw Cloyd and Walter camping on East Ute Creek far below. I could almost see the entrance to the lost gold mine on the ridge above the creek. And I could imagine Cloyd with the two grizzly cubs, Brownie and Cocoa, as the snow was starting to fall. I practically ran home, my head bursting with ideas for the story. I poured all of my love of the mountains and of bears into the writing, as well as my deep respect for native traditions.[40]

Will Hobbs has always had a deep love for adventuring into the wild places of the world and many of his books are centered on environmental themes. He has said, "I'd like my readers to appreciate and care more about what's happening to wild creatures, wild places, and the diversity of life."

As for the 10 chapters he had already written, Hobbs says, "I tossed them away. Now I knew they didn't belong. The sequel should begin with Cloyd and Walter riding into the mountains in pursuit of the treasure. I started over. I found my fingers flying all day and into the night. In writing, as in reading, you're imagining what it's like to be someone else, and I was fully imagining being Cloyd Atcitty, at 11,800 feet, with winter coming on, risking his life for those grizzly cubs. I completed an all-new version of the novel in less than a month. It was a wonderful experience, and I don't know if one like it will ever come again."[41]

In **The Big Wander**, *14-year-old Clay searches for his lost uncle, a former rodeo star, in the deserts and canyons of Utah. As with all of his books, Will Hobbs likes to visit the areas he writes about to do thorough research. Here, his wife, Jean, hikes along the Escalante River in Utah.*

4

Writing with
the Five Senses

WILL HOBBS'S BOOK *The Big Wander* is inspired by the life of Everett Ruess, a poet and artist who, as a very young man, spent parts of five years roaming the wilderness regions of Utah, Arizona, California, and Colorado. Ruess searched for beauty during his travels with a burro and dog named Curly. He found it in the fishing shacks of Sausalito, California; the peaks and mesas of Monument Valley in Utah; and the rugged rock formations of the Tsegi Canyon in Arizona.

Ruess wrote in a letter to a friend while camping on Navajo Mountain in Utah:

A high wind is roaring in the tops of the tall pines . . . The moon is just rising on the rim of the desert, far below. Stars gleam through the pine boughs and the filmy clouds that move across the night sky. Graceful, slim-trunked aspens reach upward under the towering pines. Their slender, curving branches are white in the firelight, and an occasional downward breeze flickers their pale green leaves.[42]

Hobbs admires Ruess's letters, collected after he died, not only because the young explorer possessed the spirit of the wilderness adventurer. Clearly, he also admires Ruess for his gift of prose. Ruess had the ability to impart a genuine sense for what it is like to hike through the landscape of the Southwest, camp under the radiant full moon that shines over the desert, and smell the aspen trees as they bloom in the spring.

Ruess disappeared in 1934 at the age of 20 while wandering through the canyons near the Escalante River in Utah. He left behind paintings, prints made from woodcuts, photographs, poems, and letters. His work detailed what he saw during his five years of wandering. Before he disappeared, Ruess wrote, "Much of the time I feel so exuberant I can hardly contain myself. The colors are so glorious, the forests so magnificent, the mountains so splendid, and the streams so utterly, wildly, tumultuously, effervescently joyful that to me, at least, the world is a riot of . . . delight."[43]

Everett Ruess wrote with his five senses. He used his eyes, ears, nose, taste, and sense of touch to absorb everything around him and relay it to his readers. That is the type of writing that Hobbs had adopted for his own stories.

In *The Big Wander*, which was published in 1992, Hobbs's character, Clay Lancaster, has the same love of life and nature as Everett Ruess; however, Hobbs made substantial changes to his character. Clay is 14 years old and the story is set in

1962—the same year Hobbs was 14. "I didn't want to write Everett's story," says Hobbs. "I wanted to make up a story that would be a tip of the hat to him. I decided to set the story in the summer of 1962. My main character is fourteen that summer, just like I was. There's a lot of me in Clay Lancaster."[44]

Hobbs also gave Clay a far different mission than Ruess's search for the beauty of the American Southwest. In *The Big Wander*, Clay searches for a lost uncle who is a former rodeo star. Accompanied only by a burro and a dog named Curly, Clay searches through forests, deserts, and rocky canyons while enduring the harsh elements of the wilderness.

The Big Wander serves as a textbook example of how Hobbs writes a book. For starters, Hobbs spent months researching the life of Everett Ruess. Hobbs read Ruess's letters, examined his artwork, and read books that were written about his life. Of course, Hobbs personally visited many of the scenes that he would describe in the book, including the canyons of the Escalante River and the old wagon trail blazed by the Mormon pioneers. For the character of Clay Lancaster, Hobbs borrowed largely from himself. "The part about how he acts around girls, for one thing," Hobbs says. "I was a romantic, but shy just like Clay. And, like Clay, I was a younger brother. This story has the feel of one particular road trip on Route 66 with my brother Ed. We came across the 'baby rattlers' at the trading post, just like in the novel. I would have given anything to have had all the rest of those adventures I cooked up for Clay."[45] Other characters in *The Big Wander* were drawn from traits of people whom Hobbs has known. The character of the young girl named Sarah who rescues Clay from quicksand was inspired by Hobbs's niece Sarah.

Finally, just before he was ready to start writing *The Big Wander*, Hobbs composed an outline for the book. For a typical outline, Hobbs puts down on paper how he expects the story to begin, how he expects the story to unfold, how the characters will react to one another, and how the story will end. He also spends time writing sketches about each character. He describes in notes to himself not only the physical qualities of each character, but also their personalities. In the book *Downriver*, which featured seven young people on a survival trip through the wilderness, Hobbs says he wrote "pages and pages on each one before I ever started writing the story."[46]

Did you know...

Even though Will Hobbs based the character of Clay Lancaster on the poet and artist Everett Ruess, Hobbs borrowed a lot from his own life—including the scene in *The Big Wander* when Clay chews up his ticket to the dance.

In the book, Clay is nervously waiting in line and absent-mindedly puts his ticket into his mouth. By the time he reaches the ticket-taker, Clay can't find his ticket and suddenly remembers that it's in his mouth, chewed into a soggy ball.

Hobbs admits to a similar experience when he was young. "Once I bought a ticket for a movie and then stood in line with my friends waiting for the doors to open," he recalls. "When I finally got to the ticket-taker, I realized I had been chewing on my ticket. It was now a spitwad."[*]

[*] "Favorite Questions about Will," Will Hobbs Official Website, *www.willhobbsauthor.com/questions.html*.

The character descriptions can be quite extensive. Hobbs says he includes "the way they talk, what they would wear, the kind of music they would listen to, the kind of friends they would have, what sorts of trouble they would have gotten into—just kind of jamming on ideas about everything on that kid."[47] In *Downriver*, Hobbs says:

> One character started from a newspaper clipping. More often I start with a kid I've taught, or some distinctive personality characteristic in a person I know. Sometimes I draw on adults. To create a character, I take several people, mixing and matching, and make up the rest.[48]

Once Hobbs finishes the outline, he typically sets it aside and writes a new one.

"For *The Big Wander*, I probably had 10 different outlines before I made myself start writing," he says:

> I would sleep on each one, thinking it was wonderful, but I would always awake perceiving some flaw. Finally, I sat down and started writing a scene. Two brothers were on the road, in an old Studebaker truck on old Route 66 in 1962. They were making a stop at a tourist trap. Things started happening, as they always do once the subconscious is engaged, that I never could have foreseen in an outline. Once you're imagining being that main character, and you're having the conversations and actually being there, the magic in fiction writing takes over. Some of the best things that have happened in my stories have happened seemingly of their own accord. The writer becomes a listener, just writing things down as they come.[49]

In fact, Hobbs says, he has stuck closely to the outlines for very few books. Sometimes he finds the story moving in an unanticipated direction and just lets himself follow the events as they unravel. Many of his best ideas come as he imagines being the character in a certain situation. In some cases, he may have left something out of the outline that he knows he wants to include in the book, but can't imagine how it will fit. So he keeps that information in his head and, when the opportunity presents itself, he adds it to the book. That's what happened in *The Big Wander*. He says,

> The ideas I jot down during my reading, in the research phase prior to writing, often provide possibilities for the story, but I don't know at what point in the story they'll be useful. When I was reading for *The Big Wander*, for example, I found two books on burros. One had a photo of a burro inside a house, and the other had a photo of a baby burro in a backpack. I stuck two notes on my bulletin board: "Get a burro inside a house" and "Get a baby burro inside a backpack." I began the story not knowing how to make those things happen, but I kept my eye out for the time and place to make them happen, and in both cases the story steered in their direction.[50]

The baby burro, which Clay names "Burrito," does indeed make it into Clay's backpack. In the story, Clay has just helped with the delivery of the baby burro. Now, a day later, he wants to continue his journey, but doesn't know how he can return to the trail while burdened with a newborn baby burro. Here is how Hobbs has Clay solve the problem:

> He wanted to find his way out of the canyon and up onto the open country above. That wasn't going to be easy, especially with the baby burro. Burrito didn't seem to be able to predict which way his legs were going to go.

The backpack! I'll bet he'd fit in the backpack!

When Clay was all set to go, he tried it. Sure enough, Burrito made a perfect fit. Clay shouldered the pack; it was quite a sensation to look out of the corner of your eye and see that snug face and those ears. Burrito's legs were held so snugly, he didn't even bother to kick.[51]

As Hobbs explained in the case of *Beardance*, if he is not convinced that the story is working he will set aside a manuscript that represents weeks or even months of writing. Usually, when an author decides to take such dramatic measures, there is something that is deeply wrong with the story that can't easily be fixed. Indeed, every manuscript is imperfect in some way. Many authors, Hobbs included, will write numerous drafts and constantly revise their words until they get the story to come out the way they want. For Hobbs, most of the work of revising has to do with adding emotion as well as detail and color to his scenes.

For example, here is a scene from an early draft of *Bearstone*, in which Hobbs describes how Cloyd takes out his anger on Walter by slicing through the bark of the old man's peach trees:

He made a cut in the dozen or so peach trees, about a third of the way through. He didn't want them to die. He just wanted the leaves to wither and yellow, and the peaches to shrivel.[52]

That paragraph provides a lot of information, to be sure, but Hobbs believed he could do more with it. He was sure he could describe the scene in a way that would enable the reader to imagine himself right there in the peach grove with Cloyd, watching the Ute boy slice the trees. Here is how the

paragraph read in the final draft of *Bearstone*, after Hobbs
made several revisions:

> He cut through the skin of the nearest tree and winced as he
> withdrew the saw. Beads of moisture were forming along the
> edges of the fresh wound. From one to the next he ran with the
> saw roaring at full throttle, and he cut each of the twenty-two
> peach trees most of the way through. Each time, as the saw's
> teeth bit into the thin bark, he hollered with hurt as if he felt
> the saw himself. He didn't want to cut them down, he wanted
> them to die slowly. Before they died, their leaves would
> yellow and the peaches shrivel, and they would look just like
> his grandmother's peaches.[53]

What is the difference between the two versions of this
scene? Hobbs asks.

> In the first version, the narrator mostly *tells* us that Cloyd
> cut the trees. In the second, the narrator *shows* it. Showing
> means using the five senses as you write. Everything we
> experience comes to us through our senses. When I wrote
> the first version of this scene, I assumed that Cloyd's
> cutting the peach trees would show his anger, without
> telling it. But in the first version, the reader cannot become
> very involved. Most of us have heard the sound a chainsaw
> makes, for example, but does the first version bring that
> vivid sound to mind? In the second version, we're in
> Cloyd's shoes, experiencing this awful moment through
> his senses. We see the teeth of the chain biting into the
> thin bark of the peach trees. We see the little beads of sap
> forming. We see and feel the cut as a wound in a living
> thing. Implicitly, we feel the saw in our own hands and
> feel the vibration running through our bodies. We hear the

saw "roaring at full throttle." We hear Cloyd hollering with hurt, and it feels as if we are hollering, too.[54]

Hobbs seeks other opinions for his manuscripts, as many writers do. Even after spending a considerable time conceiving the story, drawing images of the characters, working on outlines, and then, finally, writing and rewriting the manuscript, the book may still not be ready for publication. Many times, another set of eyes will uncover problems in the manuscript the author may have missed.

For example, the order in which the author has linked the events together may not make sense. Perhaps a character's motivations may not be fully clear to the reader. Perhaps the author may have chosen words the reader does not understand. That is an important consideration when the book is intended for a young audience. Perhaps the problem simply comes down to the author not doing his best work. In many cases, an editor who works for the book's publisher will read the manuscript and return it to the author for revision. Hobbs says he has learned to rely on his editor's judgment. "Usually, my editor in New York helps me by telling me which parts of the story are working well and which parts I should go back and work on some more," says Hobbs. "Most of the time I'll have three drafts before I'm finished."[55]

For Hobbs, writing is work but it is also a pleasure. When Hobbs writes, he can look out a window at the countryside of southwestern Colorado. His backyard includes a wide view of the Weminuche Wilderness—the same area explored by Cloyd and Walter in *Bearstone* and *Beardance*. If, while he is writing, Hobbs finds himself in need of a moment of inspiration, he need only look up from his desk. He'll see mountain peaks, wildflowers, and wildlife. "As I write, sometimes there's a herd of elk gazing right outside

When Will Hobbs works in his home in Durango, Colorado, he can look out the window and see mountain peaks, wildflowers, and wildlife for inspiration. "As I write, sometimes there's a herd of elk grazing right outside my window."

the window," he says.[56] "Out my windows I see cliffs where falcons nest, and high mountain peaks that are white with snow about seven months out of the year."[57]

Actually, before he sits down to write each day, Hobbs follows one tiny rule he set for himself long ago. Sitting on his desk is a small toy pterodactyl, a flying prehistoric reptile. Just before he is ready to write, Hobbs winds up the toy and watches it waddle across his desk. By the time the pterodactyl reaches the other side of his desk, he must start writing. Says Hobbs, "I owe about three books, especially *Beardance*, to that little guy. I might have given up if it hadn't been for my deal with the pterodactyl."[58]

It usually takes Hobbs a year to finish a book. He doesn't work on the book full time during that period. Hobbs will take time off for travel and making speeches before conferences of teachers and librarians, who are, after all, very important to the success of his books. He also does public readings of new books at bookstores and in front of school audiences. When he sits behind his desk in his Durango home to write, he usually works from 9 A.M. until 5 P.M. Except for minor interruptions such as retrieving the mail or making himself a cup of coffee, Hobbs pretty much commits himself to his work for the day. He says, "I can build up more intensity if I work all day long. If the story is really cooking, I'll go back to my study in the evenings."[59]

As a teenager, Hobbs generally didn't write unless he was required to submit an essay or a book report as a school assignment. Hobbs believes young people who want to be writers should be readers first and foremost. Then they should begin putting their thoughts down on paper as soon as they feel inspired. He says they should not wait for a teacher to make them write as an assignment.

Hobbs has some advice for young writers. He says:

> Write! You get better by doing it. Get a rough draft written that you can work with, and revise it later. Find a partner who also likes to write and read each other's stuff, provide encouragement, make suggestions. Remember that both readers and writers are imagining what it's like to be someone else, so write with the five senses. Let your readers hear, see, smell, touch and taste what your characters are experiencing.[60]

In Will Hobbs's book Downriver, *Jessie is a troubled teenage girl who gains a new sense of responsibility on a wilderness survival trip on the Colorado River. Here, Hobbs demonstrates that he knows first-hand about white-water rafting on a trip through the Grand Canyon.*

5

Taking the Big Waves

JESSIE ISN'T A bad girl. She just has a bit of wildness in her. She hasn't broken the law or lived in the streets, like some of her friends in Will Hobbs's book *Downriver*. Instead, Jessie is just a bit too much for her widower father to handle. So he sends her off to a wilderness survival program named Discovery Unlimited or, as the teenagers call it, "Hoods in the Woods." At the camp, Jessie is expected to learn how to climb mountains, build cooking fires, and raft through dangerous river rapids. She is also expected to learn about teamwork and how to appreciate other people's needs.

Jessie is less than enthusiastic about the program. She complains early in the book:

> He was sending me away . . . No matter how much he denied it, that's what he was doing, and I threw it back in his face a hundred times. He just wanted to believe the therapist, who told him this is what I needed—to discover myself, learn my limits, all that psych talk. It just made him feel better about getting rid of me.[61]

Hobbs's first two books, *Changes in Latitudes* and *Bearstone*, featured boys as the main characters. In *Downriver* Hobbs makes the main character a troubled teenage girl; however, he keeps all the other elements of his fiction. *Downriver*'s characters are challenged on an adventure in the wilderness. The story takes them through a landscape of incredible beauty. They find themselves battling for survival against the elements. And finally, the main character rises up and becomes a leader. She recognizes her strengths and weaknesses, as well as those in others.

Hobbs always intended to make the main character of *Downriver* a girl, but his original character was a completely different type of girl than Jessie. The original girl from his first draft did not end up in the story. In the second draft, Hobbs made the narrator a boy; however, in the third draft, when he created Jessie, he knew he had found his female protagonist.

> It was partly because it was the next challenge for me as a writer, to imagine the world from a girl's point of view, but mostly because I thought that outdoor adventure novels needed to catch up to real life. Outdoor adventure is every bit as appealing to girls as it is to boys. Just look around at who's out there—skiing, mountain biking, kayaking, river rafting,

climbing. Girls are active in every kind of sport. On our own hikes and river trips we see at least as many girls as boys.[62]

There is little question that for more than a century, girls have been underrepresented as the protagonists in not only adventure stories, but in most types of young people's fiction that includes any sort of physical danger, mystery, action, or sport. Certainly, there are exceptions. Scott O'Dell's 1960 novel, *Island of the Blue Dolphins*, tells the story of Karana, a young Indian girl who battles the elements to stay alive on a remote island.

Perhaps the most famous of all female protagonists is Nancy Drew, a teenage detective who began solving mysteries in the 1920s. Nancy is bright, attractive, talented, and independent. She drives a sports car. Her boyfriend is on the football team. In other words, Nancy Drew is the type of girl every one of her fans wishes they could be. Still, Nancy doesn't seem to be the type of girl willing to break a nail to solve a crime. "She is an artifact of gentility, of primness, of an era when villains posed as members of the household staff to steal a family heirloom and girl detectives made sure their shoes and pocketbooks matched," critic Amy Benfer has said.[63]

Indeed, Nancy may be able to solve crimes, but when it comes to the rough stuff she is always thankful when her boyfriend Ned Nickerson is handy to break down a door. Author Bobbie Ann Mason, who examined the popularity of Nancy Drew and other girl detectives in her book *The Girl Sleuth*, points out that Nancy is sometimes made to feel like a second-class citizen. In other words, she is told that she is "just a girl." As for Nancy, she often accepts her role not with reluctance but with delight. Mason points out that in one of Nancy's adventures, *The Haunted Bridge*, the female

detective is called on to help a doctor remove a bullet frag-
ment from a shooting victim. The operation is successful. The
doctor tells Nancy that he appreciated her assistance:

> "Have you ever studied nursing?" he asked Nancy abruptly.
> "Oh, no, I've had only training in first aid."
> "You seem to have missed your calling," the doctor told her
> with a smile. "You appear to have a natural bent for nursing."
> Nancy flushed with pride.[64]

Mason says that it never occurred to the doctor—or to
Nancy herself—that she might have a future as a doctor,
not a nurse. Writes Mason, "If girls cannot aspire to
important careers in medicine and law and business, they
can be rewarded for assisting men."[65]

Hobbs says he recognized a need for a strong female
character in young people's adventure fiction years ago
while working as a teacher.

> When I was a reading teacher, I had five hundred books in my
> classroom. Typically, the adventure books had boy protago-
> nists. With *Downriver*, I wanted to write from the point of view
> of a girl. I wanted to turn the genre on its head and have the girl
> be the main character. I was trying to create a convincing
> feminine sensibility—a sense of what girls are really like.[66]

In *Downriver*, Jessie goes along with a scheme with six
other teens to steal a van and sneak off on a white-water
rafting trip down the Colorado River. At first, she lets the boys
run things. She is satisfied merely to sit in the boat, watch
the scenery go by, and concentrate on her crush on Troy.

> I loved being in the front of the boat, taking all the big
> waves, and looking back to Troy at work on the oars. He

really loved the white water. In the rapids he wore a wonderful grin all over his face, and his blue eyes were all concentration looking downstream. He was learning how to move the boat, how to spin it to avoid the rocks and holes. He was learning when to apply power and when to apply finesse.

I watched the runs the paddle raft was making behind us as well. I heard Adam saying that as long as he kept the boat straight, they could blow through the holes, and that's what they were doing, going intentionally for the action.[67]

Of course, things soon start going wrong. Troy turns out to be a jerk, and the other boys are reluctant to challenge his destructive leadership. Late in the book, Freddy is stung by a scorpion. To save his life, the teenagers must break away from Troy and paddle their boat through a treacherous stretch of rapids known as "Upset." By this point, Jessie emerges as the only one remaining who is capable of leading the group. She willingly takes charge, maps out a strategy, and prepares to lead the others through the rapids.

We rounded a bend and came into the sunshine at last. Within moments I was warm. I felt good. I felt strong. I can do it, I told myself. Blue skies ahead; it won't be the kind of day we had at Crystal. I'll scout the rapid and I'll find a way and I'll bring them through to Havasu. Ten miles up the trail to the Supai village.[68]

Jessie doesn't get the chance to lead her friends out of the wilderness. Just before arriving at the Upset the teens are spotted by a helicopter, which collects them and flies Freddy to safety. However, Jessie returns to her father a much different person. She is more responsible and, above all, anxious for new adventures in the wilderness. "There will be other tests as important for me, maybe not as physical, but I'll recognize them when I see them and apply my Upset strategy," she says.[69]

That opportunity soon arrives. Hobbs followed up *Downriver* with its sequel, *River Thunder*. In the second book, the Hoods in the Woods characters return for another trip down the Colorado River. Again, Jessie must step forward and be the leader. In *River Thunder*, Hobbs says he wanted to make Jessie even more independent. That is why Hobbs didn't include Freddy in the sequel. Until he was bitten by a scorpion in *Downriver*, Freddy had proven to be the most reliable of the boys. Says Hobbs, "It all has to do with Jessie. If she has to deal with Troy and the river without Freddy, she comes into her own. Freddy is not there to pull everyone's fat out of the fire."[70]

Hobbs wanted *Downriver* and *River Thunder* to be about more than just a modern girl coming into her own. He wanted to explore friendships among young people and show how relationships change as people learn more about one another. For example, early in *Downriver* Hobbs portrays Troy as a leader. He is intelligent and good-looking and Jessie finds herself drawn to him. Later, Troy's true character is revealed. Says Hobbs:

> I'd had some experience with a kid a lot like Troy, and wanted to dramatize just how much power an appealing but manipulative leader can have on a group. The other kids trust him in the beginning, and Jessie is quite taken with him. As the dangers of their situation become clearer to them, each of those seven kids who are on their own will need to start thinking for themselves, figuring out who to listen to, who to trust.[71]

Hobbs also wanted to write about the action and dangers of white-water rafting down the Colorado River and through the Grand Canyon. Hobbs and his wife Jean have rafted through the Grand Canyon numerous times themselves and they know how exciting it can be. Says Hobbs, "Running the Colorado River through the Grand Canyon is sometimes called the great American adventure."[72]

Did you know...

Will Hobbs had his first experience white-water rafting in 1979 accompanying Brent Brown, a fellow teacher at Miller Junior High School in Durango, on a trip down the Dolores River in Colorado and Utah.

"One taste, and Jean and I became serious river rats," says Hobbs. "Most years we would spend thirty days on rivers—canyon rivers in the Southwest and also the Salmon River in Idaho. We rafted the Grand Canyon for the first time in the high water of 1983, and had the time of our lives."[*]

Hobbs says he and his wife have rafted the Colorado River through the Grand Canyon another nine times in the past two decades. "We could never get enough of its whitewater and its beauty," he says. "Once, we even did it solo, just the two of us."[**]

[*] Peacock, Scot, ed. *Something About the Author.* vol. 127. Farmington Hills, M.I.: Gale Group, 2002.

[**] Ibid.

Certainly, Hobbs brought his own experiences to *Downriver* and *River Thunder*, but he also read extensively about the adventures of John Wesley Powell, who first navigated the Colorado River in 1869 through what would become known as the Grand Canyon. Powell's book, *Down the Colorado: Diary of the First Trip Through the Grand Canyon*, proved to be a valuable resource to Hobbs. In his diary, Powell talked about the dangers and thrills of navigating the Colorado River rapids:

> The waves caused by such [rapids] in a river differ much from the waves of the sea. The water of an ocean wave merely rises and falls . . . . But here, the water . . . plunges down ten or twenty feet [and] springs up again in a great wave; then down and up, in a series of billows, that gradually disappear in the more quiet waters below . . . . A boat riding such, leaps and plunges along with great velocity. Now, the difficulty in riding over these [rapids], when the rocks are out of the way, is in the first wave . . . . This will sometimes gather for a moment, heaping up higher and higher, until it breaks back. If the boat strikes it the instant after it breaks, she cuts through, and the mad breaker dashes its spray over the boat, and would wash us overboard if we did not cling tight.[73]

More than a century later, Hobbs put Jessie and her friends through a similar experience.

> . . . when we went up onto a big wave sideways, I got thrown out. One instant I was paddling, trying to do what I could do to straighten the boat, and the next I was suddenly in that freezing green and white water. It was an overwhelming shock to find myself outside the boat and in the river. It

could have been a whole lot worse, though. Fortunately, as I was flying out I'd grabbed the chicken line that ran around the boat and was holding on for dear life. I was only out for a few seconds, as it turned out. Star, of all people, did exactly what Al had taught us to do. She reached over my back and grabbed the bottom of my life jacket in one hand, the shoulder of my jacket with the other, and pulled me back into the boat like a tuna fisherman pulling a big one out of the sea.[74]

In *River Thunder*, the teenagers encounter an even more exciting and dangerous run of rapids. Located upstream from the Grand Canyon is a huge reservoir known as Lake Powell. Releases from the lake into the Colorado River are controlled by the Glen Canyon Dam. In 1983, when Hobbs and Jean made their first rafting trip down the Colorado, a tremendous amount of water was released from the lake to compensate for an overfilled reservoir above. People rafting down the river, including Hobbs and Jean, were caught in the huge surge of water. "It was a heady time for rafter, private and professional alike, who happened to be on the river," Hobbs recalls.

Helicopters were flying up and down the canyon, dropping messages on unsuspecting boaters, warning them about the rising water and advising them to seek higher ground. . . . On our '83 trip, I was rowing a fifteen-foot raft, often through waves more than twenty feet high. Our rafts were rowed by four men and one woman, only two of whom had rowed the canyon before. We managed to complete the trip with only two flips among us, a result that gave me confidence that Jessie and Troy's combined total of three flips in the novel was realistic.[75]

The Maze *is the story of Rick Walter, who, while lost in Canyonlands National Park, becomes involved in a mission to release endangered California condors back into the wild. Here, Will Hobbs is pictured resting from his hike above Canyonlands in Utah.*

Hobbs recreates those conditions in *River Thunder*. He sends Jessie and the others through the rapids at Lava Falls. They flip over—"simply buried with whitewater, but they come through unscathed," he says.[76]

As for the rest of the journey down the Colorado River, Hobbs says anybody making the trip today can be assured they will experience it all just as Jessie experiences it in *Downriver* and *River Thunder*. Says Hobbs:

> If Jessie talks about the poison ivy at a certain location, it's really there. It was great fun for me to describe the amazing attractions down there, like the side stream called the Little Colorado, which Jessie names the River of Blue. I made the song of the canyon wren a sort of theme in *Downriver* and a strong touchpoint between Jessie and Star, who become very close. Friendship is a big part of this story.[77]

Will Hobbs's book Kokopelli's Flute *is an adventure story that incorporates myths of the ancient Anasazi Indians, native to the southwestern United States. He researched the book by exploring the wilderness areas and visiting Indian archeological sites in New Mexico. Here, Hobbs is pictured with his niece, Sarah.*

6

The Magical and the Mysterious

WHEN HOBBS PLANNED his book *Kokopelli's Flute*, he knew he wanted his readers to learn about the magical powers of Kokopelli, the mythical humpbacked figure who is said to have wandered the Southwest giving seeds to Indian villages and summoning rain to help their crops grow. He intended for *Kokopelli's Flute* to be an adventure story. Hobbs's main character, a nonnative boy named Tepary Jones, is entranced with a nearby cliff dwelling, abandoned long ago by the Anasazi, the ancestors of today's Pueblo Indians. Over the course of the story, Tep catches a group of thieves stealing

Anasazi artifacts and finds the medicine that will save his mother's life.

Hobbs's challenge was to figure out how to knit together an ancient legend with a modern adventure story. "I needed, early on, to let the reader know that this is fantasy," says Hobbs.

> After all, we're going to meet a character who is thousands of years old. Well, I didn't know how I was going to deal with this. Right when I needed an answer, I had a lucky accident. My pickup truck hadn't been running very well, so I drove it into town and asked my mechanic to take a look at it. As soon as he popped the hood he started laughing. My motor was covered with a huge nest made out of sticks, bones, rocks and weeds! 'You've got packrats!' he announced, still laughing. A light bulb went on in my head. Here was the key to my story. You see, I knew that packrats lived in the cliff ruins all over the Southwest. My character, Tep, could be visiting his favorite cliff during an eclipse of the moon, and something magical would happen to him. After he plays the ancient flute, every night he turns into a packrat![78]

And that is how the story unfolds. After thwarting the theft of some Anasazi artifacts, Tep finds a flute carved from bone. Whenever he plays the flute, he turns into a bushy-tailed pack rat.

> I remember putting the flute to my lips and blowing on it a minute or two. The notes I was producing sounded as pure as falling water. I remember starting to feel dizzy . . . the room started spinning and reeling, and I was bucking like I was being ripped open and turned inside out. Next thing I knew, I had the sensation of having long black whiskers radiating

out from my face. These whiskers almost hurt, they were so sensitive. My nose was twitching. I was aware of an alien scent, musky, overpowering, and close.[79]

Kokopelli's Flute marked a new direction for Hobbs's literature. Until then, every story Hobbs wrote was realistic fiction. To give his stories their authenticity, he insisted on hiking the trails his characters hiked. He rafted the river rapids his characters rafted, and climbed the mountains his characters climbed. While *Kokopelli's Flute* is fantasy, Hobbs insisted on thorough research before beginning to write the book. He visited a seed farm in New Mexico. Having long been interested in the culture of the Anasazi Indians he expanded his knowledge of their history. In these ways Hobbs was able to ground the myth and magic in *Kokopelli's Flute* with a realistic feel and foundation, an important trait of good fantasy.

Kokopelli's Flute, which was published in 1995, and another book, *Ghost Canoe*, published two years later, constitute Hobbs's two departures from the adventure genre. To be sure, both books contain elements of adventure, but *Kokopelli's Flute* belongs in the category of fantasy fiction, while *Ghost Canoe* is a mystery. *Ghost Canoe*, which is set in 1874, follows Nathan MacAllister, the 14-year-old son of a lighthouse keeper, as he unravels a murder on Washington state's Olympic Peninsula. Along the way, Nathan learns the ways of the Makah Indian tribe. As is typical among Hobbs's characters, Nathan survives a battle against the elements and learns much about Native American culture. Still, the heart of the story is Nathan's pursuit of the murderer of a ship's captain.

When Hobbs decided to branch out into the fantasy and mystery genres, he joined two very crowded fields. Readers searching for stories written by contemporary mystery authors can find dozens of books on the shelves written by such popular writers as Wendelin Van Draanen, author of the Sammy Keyes series of mysteries, and the late Joan Lowery Nixon, who wrote more than 140 novels for young readers before her death in 2003.

Even more competitive than the mystery genre is the category of books that explores the worlds of myth. Among the most popular young people's books today are the stories in the *Lord of the Rings* series, which includes books written decades ago by South African-born author J.R.R. Tolkien. The *Lord of the Rings* trilogy tells the adventures of a band of heroes who battle a wicked sorcerer as they try to bring peace to the mythical land of Middle Earth. Also setting sales records are the adventures of Harry Potter. By 2004, the five books featuring the boy wizard sold some 250 million copies worldwide.

Hobbs says he found *Kokopelli's Flute* and *Ghost Canoe* among his easiest books to write. "I was able to let my imagination run riot while largely sticking to my outlines— an unusual combination."[80] For his other books, Hobbs always followed his outlines loosely, but he would often let the story take over and go in an unplanned direction. However, with these two books, Hobbs found that he had to plan out more of his story line in advance, and stick to the outline more closely. When Tep is trapped in the body of the packrat every night, Hobbs had to know how and where his nighttime forays would steer the plot, and once the sea captain's body washes ashore in *Ghost Canoe,* readers expect Nathan to solve the mystery.

Indeed, *Ghost Canoe* gave Hobbs few opportunities to restructure the story once he started writing. Mysteries are usually planned in reverse. Before the writer begins, he

Did you know...

When writing *Ghost Canoe*, Will Hobbs made use of a dictionary of the Chinook Indian language he obtained while visiting the Olympic Peninsula in Washington. In the book, Nathan MacAllister learns some Chinook terms from Lighthouse George, a Makah Indian.

The Makahs also have their own language. One of the challenges facing Makah leaders is preservation of the language, which is known as Qwiqwidicciat. The language is believed to be more than a thousand years old, but today few members of the tribe speak it fluently.

Most of the best speakers of the language are elderly, which means that tribal leaders are in a race against time to save the language. In 2002, tribal elder Ruth Claplanhoo died at the age of 100. She was the last Makah who learned to speak Qwiqwidicciat as a mother tongue, meaning she spoke Qwiqwidicciat before she learned English. Janine Bowechop, executive director of the Makah Cultural and Resource Center, told a news reporter, "It's devastating. There are some things that will be forever lost. You see a lot in a hundred years, and build a lot of character and a lot of wisdom."[*]

To help preserve Qwiqwidicciat, the tribe has established the Makah Language Program. Volunteers work with older members of the tribe, recording oral histories. Tribe members are also preparing a dictionary that will translate Qwiqwidicciat into English.

[*] Barber, Mike. "Basket Weaver's Legacy is Woven into Fabric of the Makah." *Seattle Post-Intelligencer*, August 22, 2002.

must decide who will be the culprit and how the crime will be committed. Next, he must plan backwards by thinking of clues to leave the reader. This is the process Hobbs found himself using with *Ghost Canoe*. When it came time to write the book Hobbs had to discipline himself to stay within the outline. Hobbs says:

> You have to have your act together to write a mystery . . . You know who the bad guy is and you have to plan for clues. With a mystery, you have to look deep into your plot and get it figured out. Usually with outlines, I know where I want to go but I don't know how to get there. I often end up going in a route I didn't imagine. The mystery was an exception. I was able to write the outline and stick with it.[81]

With the extensive preparation for *Kokopelli's Flute* and *Ghost Canoe* finished, the writing part turned out to be the easiest part of the job for Hobbs. It was simply a matter of filling in the story.

Although the two books are not typical Will Hobbs adventures, he still added to the stories some of the familiar elements that his readers have come to expect. Hobbs says he decided to write *Kokopelli's Flute* because, as he hiked and explored the Southwest, he would constantly see images of Kokopelli carved into cliff walls, boulders, and pueblo dwellings by Native American artists. "I've always been fascinated with the magic flute player, Kokopelli," says Hobbs.

> The ancient people of the Americas chipped his picture into the rocks all the way from Peru to Colorado. Hiking in remote canyons, I would often come across Kokopelli on cliff walls. I knew that the modern pueblo people of the Southwest, including the Hopi of Arizona, say that the hump on

Kokopelli's back is a bag of seeds that he would bring to the villages scattered far and wide. His magic flute brought the rain necessary to sprout the seeds. One day, staring at one of these pictures in stone, I got to daydreaming. What if Kokopelli is still alive, I thought. He's thousands of years old, but he's still alive! What if I were to write a story in which he comes into the life of a modern kid? Wow![82]

In the story, Tep and his family nurture rare native seeds to ensure the crops do not fall into extinction. From time to time, a mysterious man sends them new seeds to nurture. They know this mysterious seed provider as "Mister K."

All our crops were dry-farmed, which means we never irrigated them. The idea was to plant rare vegetable seeds that can thrive in places where there is hardly any rain, and to produce a whole lot more drought-resistant seeds for people who subscribe to our catalog. My dad was all excited about a package of seeds he'd received the day before from Mister K.

We didn't have any idea who'd been sending us the seeds all this time because Mister K. never gave a name or a return address. My father guessed that he was a famous botanist who cherished his privacy—maybe a retired university professor. Whoever he was, he had a lot in common with the hump-backed flute player of ancient times, the legendary long-distance traveler who brought seeds from place to place. So my father dubbed him "Mister K." in Kokopelli's honor.[83]

Kokopelli's Flute follows Tep's thirteenth summer growing up in a remote part of New Mexico. Eventually, the mysterious Mister K. will walk into the seed farm and Tep's life. The story covers a lot of territory, including the importance of seed farming, the ways of life of the Anasazi

Indians, the threat to Anasazi sites posed by thieves who steal artifacts from burial places, and the horrors of the disease known as hantavirus.

"Hantavirus is very real," notes Hobbs. "Right when I was writing the book, the newspapers were full of stories about people in the Four Corners area of Colorado, New Mexico, Arizona and Utah dying from it. It's carried by deer mice and it's very scary."[84]

Hantavirus, a disease spread by the deer mouse, was first discovered in the United States in 1993. Humans contract the disease by breathing in air that carries tiny particles of urine and droppings left by the rodents. The virus can also be spread if a person is bitten by a rodent that is carrying the disease. The virus attacks the lungs, causing them to fill with fluid. The victims suffer shortness of breath as well as fever and deep muscle aches. It is often fatal. According to the U.S. Centers for Disease Control and Prevention, in 1995—the year *Kokopelli's Flute* was published—there were two fatal cases of hantavirus in the Four Corners states. That number increased to 14 by 1998. The disease may be rare, but people who live in the Four Corners area have been advised by public health officials to keep their properties free of rodents.

In *Kokopelli's Flute*, Tep's mother contracts hantavirus. Guided by Mister K., Tep uses his ability to transform into a pack rat to retrieve some ancient medicinal herbs stolen by thieves that he knows will help cure his mother. Once Tep retrieves the herbs, Mister K. brews them into a tea and serves them to Tep's mother. The cure is a success, and Mister K. disappears once more.

As with Hobbs's other stories, *Ghost Canoe* grew out of a personal experience. Hobbs traveled to the Olympic Peninsula, which is the landmass at the far northwestern

Ghost Canoe, *Will Hobbs's first mystery book, follows young Nathan MacAllister as he solves a murder in Cape Flattery, along the coast of Washington State, in 1874. Hobbs, seen here, has traveled through this rugged but beautiful area on the Olympic Peninsula near the Canadian border.*

tip of the state of Washington. The peninsula extends into the Pacific Ocean just below Vancouver Island, which is part of the Canadian province of British Columbia. At the very top of the peninsula is the Makah Indian reservation. The Makah is an ancient tribe that dates its existence back to prehistoric times. Over the years the Makahs became excellent sailors who used their skills for fishing and whaling.

Hobbs hiked through Cape Flattery, which is at the very tip of the peninsula. As he explains it,

I visited the modern Makah town of Neah Bay. I was mes-
merized by the Makah's museum, which includes countless
artifacts from a Makah village buried by mudslides in the
1400s. There, on display, was their pre-Columbian whaling
gear. Looking at those old canoes, tools, cedar boxes, fishing
gear—it all started coming to life for me. I learned that they
had hunted the great whales from their canoes well into the
twentieth century. Once I started thinking about setting a
story in the Makah's home country, I read the history of
the lighthouse on Tatoosh Island and shipwrecks nearby. I
became fascinated with the decade of the 1870s. I learned the
history of the Spanish, the British and the Americans in the
Northwest. I read voraciously about the Makahs. Of course,
my story is fictional, but it's based on history that's probably
more exciting than anything I could make up.[85]

The more Hobbs thought about it, the more it seemed his
story possibilities had all the elements of a mystery. For
years, Hobbs says, his readers had asked him to write a
mystery. Finally it seemed as though the time had arrived.
"I remembered how much I'd liked reading mysteries when
I was a kid. The combination of the lighthouse on Tatoosh
Island and a shipwreck had 'mystery' written all over it,"
he says.[86]
In the book, Nathan learns the ways of the Makahs from
Lighthouse George, a local fisherman who delivers the mail
to Nathan's father, the lighthouse keeper, in a hand-carved
canoe. With George's help, Nathan learns the art of canoe-
making as well as how to fish. "*Ghost Canoe* was inspired
by the canoes themselves," says Hobbs. "The great canoes
are once again being carved from Western red cedar trees
by native people, including the contemporary Makah, from
Washington state up through British Columbia to southeast

Alaska, and paddled on the waters of the Pacific. They are a sight to see."[87]

There is a lot for mystery fans to like in *Ghost Canoe*. Nathan finds unexplained footprints on a desolate beach. A theft occurs at the trading post. Nathan spots a wild "hairy man," which convinces him that someone is hiding in the remote sea caves along the coast. With Lighthouse George, Nathan battles against the fierce waters of the Pacific Ocean as he searches for clues.

Ghost Canoe may have been Hobbs's first mystery, but his fans eagerly embraced the story. So did the critics, and many others who enjoy reading mysteries. In 1997, the Mystery Writers of America voted it the winner of the Edgar Allan Poe Award for Best Young Adult Mystery. The award is named in honor of Poe, the nineteenth-century American poet and mystery writer. Although *Ghost Canoe* remains his only pure mystery, Hobbs found himself weaving more and more suspense into his later books. His 1998 book, *The Maze*, was not intended to be a mystery, yet the Mystery Writers of America selected it as a finalist for the Edgar Allan Poe Award. Hobbs says, "*Ghost Canoe* was my first mystery, so the Edgar came as quite a surprise to me. That award, by the way, is a small ceramic bust of Edgar Allan Poe. As I look at my more recent novels, I'm discovering that suspense and mystery are becoming stronger and stronger elements for me."[88]

In Jackie's Wild Seattle, Shannon and her brother, Cody, help their Uncle Neal, who volunteers at a Seattle wildlife rescue center. Most of the rescue stories are true stories. Will Hobbs heard the stories while doing his research at the Sarvey Wildlife Center. The part in Jackie's Wild Seattle when Uncle Neal rescues a baby bald eagle named Liberty is based on an actual incident at the center. A volunteer from the Sarvey Wildlife Center rescued a baby bald eagle named Freedom. Hobbs is pictured here with Freedom.

7

The Circle of Healing

IN HOBBS'S BOOK *Jackie's Wild Seattle*, 14-year-old Shannon Young helps her Uncle Neal capture a coyote that has somehow found its way into the elevator of an office building in downtown Seattle, Washington. Shannon and her little brother Cody are spending the summer of 2002 helping their uncle, who is a volunteer for a wildlife rescue and rehabilitation center known as "Jackie's Wild Seattle." Uncle Neal has suffered an injury to his hand. He received the wound when he was clawed by a hawk while trying to untangle the bird from a net at a golf course. Because of the injury, Uncle Neal must wear a cast. Unable to catch scared and vicious animals with just one hand, Uncle Neal has turned to Shannon and Cody to serve as his hands. In the story, workers and visitors are ordered to leave the office building. Television news crews surround the building. A big crowd forms outside. Finally, the Jackie's Wild Seattle ambulance arrives and the three rescuers get down to work.

Once in the lobby, the elevator doors are nudged open. Shannon slips into the elevator car, where she finds the frightened coyote curled up in a corner. The coyote watches her with caution. "I decided to sit down," Shannon says in the book.

> I might look less threatening that way. The coyote locked its eyes on mine as I sat cross-legged across from it. I kept talking. I explained who I was and where I was from, described our house on Liberty Street, described my room, my bedspread and everything on my dresser, then started talking about what a great city Seattle was. . . . The coyote had beautiful amber eyes. They were always right on mine.[89]

Within a few minutes, Shannon gains the trust of the coyote. The animal lets her scoop him up into her arms. She places the coyote in a small animal carrier. Later, the coyote is released in the city's waterfront area. Hobbs explains in the book that coyotes have come down from the countryside surrounding Seattle to search for food scraps left by tourists. They also hunt for mice and rats. "City rats are a menace to public health," Uncle Neal tells his niece and nephew, "which makes our urban coyotes valuable citizens."[90]

All of Hobbs's books are based in some degree on actual places, people, or events. However, no book illustrates Hobbs's literary devotion to the drama and humor of real life more than *Jackie's Wild Seattle*. For starters, the wildlife rescue service Hobbs called Jackie's Wild Seattle is based on the Sarvey Wildlife Center of Arlington, Washington. The character of Jackie, the owner of the shelter, is modeled after Kaye Baxter, who started nursing wounded wild animals back to health in the garage of her home in Everett, Washington, near Seattle. Kaye made the decision to move her clinic to the countryside when the number of animals began to overreach her capacity to care for them in a small home in her neighborhood. The animals were beginning to try the patience of her friends and neighbors in various ways. Most of the events Hobbs describes in the book are also true, including the coyote rescue in the elevator. That rescue was performed by Bob Jones, a volunteer at Sarvey. Hobbs has said that the character of Uncle Neal was partly modeled on Jones.

Hobbs says he became aware of the Sarvey Wildlife Center and its work when his brother-in-law mailed him a newspaper clipping describing the rescue of the coyote. Hobbs says:

> My brother-in-law in Seattle was aware that I'm always cutting articles out of the newspapers and magazines—just anything that catches my fancy. You never know what might turn into a story! The clipping he sent was about a volunteer for a wildlife rescue and rehab center who rescued a wild coyote from an elevator in a downtown Seattle office building. Amazingly enough, the man did it without tranquilizing the animal. He just sat down in the elevator with the coyote, talked to it, calmed it down and brought it out in a carrier. I resolved to visit the wildlife center the next time I was in the area, and to meet these amazing people.[91]

To research the book, Hobbs made several visits to the center. He spent time interviewing Kaye Baxter, Bob Jones, and the other staff members. Hobbs even traveled with the volunteers on ambulance calls. By doing that kind of firsthand research and basing his novel on actual people and events, Hobbs drew on a literary form that has been used by many authors over a number of years. The "nonfiction novel" was first popularized by the author Truman Capote, whose 1965 book *In Cold Blood* told the story of the brutal murders of a Kansas farm family. The book was based on an actual event but employed the conventions of fiction. In his book, Capote made up the dialogue and placed the words he wrote in the mouths of real people.

Another fictional account of an actual event is *Inherit the Wind*, a play written by Jerome Lawrence and Robert E. Lee in 1955 that is often taught in schools. The play tells the story of the 1925 trial of biology teacher John T. Scopes, who is charged with teaching Charles Darwin's theory of evolution in his classroom. At the time, Scopes taught evolution in defiance of the religious standards of his small Tennessee town. The "Scopes Monkey Trial" really occurred and represented an important moment in the history of education in America. The trial pitted two great lawyers of the day, William Jennings Bryan and Clarence Darrow, in a battle of wits. The trial is reenacted in *Inherit the Wind*, but Lawrence and Lee changed the names of the characters and made up the dialogue.

An example of a nonfiction novel is the book, *The Killer Angels*. The book is based on the Battle of Gettysburg and in this case, the author, Michael Shaara, doesn't change the names of his characters from those of the original people. Instead, Shaara uses the actual men and officers who fought the pivotal conflict of the Civil War as the characters for his book. Still, Shaara made up the dialogue and placed his own words in the characters' mouths.

Hobbs says the real people he found working at the Sarvey Wildlife Center served as a "jumping off point"[92] for

The character of Jackie in Jackie's Wild Seattle *is based on Kaye Baxter (pictured here with Will Hobbs), who began nursing wounded wild animals back to health in her garage in Everett, Washington, many years ago. She went on to found Sarvey Wildlife Center.*

the novel. He adds, "I'm really writing fiction and creating fictional characters. I just start with something and run with it, but I was inspired by the real people at the Sarvey Wildlife Center."[93] Even though a novel is for the most part a made-up story, Hobbs says it is the duty of fiction to inform: "The people who worked at the Sarvey Wildlife Center understood that I was a writer. They knew I would use some of what happened there, but fictionalize it."[94]

Indeed, that is what Hobbs does to a large degree in *Jackie's Wild Seattle*. Neal and Jackie are based on real people, and so are Shannon and Cody. Hobbs used characteristics of a niece and nephew to create the big sister–little brother relationship in the book. There are many scenes in the book drawn from the real adventures of the Sarvey Wildlife Center volunteers. For example, in the book, Neal, Shannon, and Cody are sent to a suburban shopping center to capture a bobcat that has been seen roaming around. Larger than house cats, bobcats live in the wild and can be vicious. Shannon takes precautions against the bobcat's attack by wearing heavy gloves. As she is poking around a trash bin behind a store, the bobcat suddenly springs at her. "It flew at me so hard I dropped the net and fell flat on my back with my hands up trying to ward it off," Shannon says. "Too late. The bobcat's front legs were locked around my neck. I was so frightened I lost control of my bladder, just peed my pants."[95]

The story is true. It happened to a local animal control officer—even the part about the unfortunate officer losing control of her bladder. The outcome of the story is also told, true to fact, in Hobbs's book. Instead of trying to hurt Shannon, the bobcat turns out to be tame and starts licking her face. It seems the bobcat, as well as its real-life counterpart, had been a house pet. In both cases, the bobcats were simply hungry. "I jumped up and the big cat rubbed back and forth against my leg, purring, like it was overjoyed I had come along," Shannon says.[96]

Despite its basis in fact, there is no question that *Jackie's Wild Seattle* is a novel. Hobbs made up the character of Tyler, the troubled boy who killed a dog and was sentenced by the court to perform community service at the animal shelter. At home, Tyler is the son of an alcoholic and abusive father. "The entire subplot about Tyler and his family is made up," says Hobbs,

> Tyler is a kid from a tough home situation. Shannon is very drawn to him. Even though her Uncle Neal warns her that he's trouble, Shannon sees the good in him. She helps him get the opportunity to care for two orphaned bear cubs at the center. Tyler grows a lot in the course of the story. He discovers his own strengths and plays a big part in the climax of the story. In real life, some of the teenagers over the years who have worked at Sarvey have been kids placed there by the courts. Helping with the animals often helps them overcome some of their own problems.[97]

Tyler isn't the only character in *Jackie's Wild Seattle* who comes to the shelter with troubles. As with most of Hobbs's stories, several characters have personal problems they must work through. Uncle Neal, for one, has just finished treatments for cancer, and he is worried that his cancer may return. But it is the character Cody who has the most pressing problems.

Hobbs wrote the book in the aftermath of the September 11, 2001, terrorist attacks on the World Trade Center in New York City and the Pentagon in Washington, D.C. He felt that it was important to make a statement about the "circle of healing."[98] That is the term used by Kaye Baxter to explain the spirit of people who devote their lives to helping others, including wildlife. In return, those people receive something back.

On the morning of September 11, Cody is on the banks of the Hudson River, not far from his home in Weehawken,

---

Did you know...

In *Jackie's Wild Seattle*, Cody Young is fascinated by natural forces that can cause disasters, such as volcanoes and hurricanes. Will Hobbs says he was the same way when he was a young boy.

Hobbs says, "Once in Virginia, and once in Texas, I wasn't far from the ocean when big hurricanes came ashore. I'll never forget the wind and the rain, and how so many turtles were flushed out. I'm still fascinated and awed by the power of volcanoes, hurricanes, tornadoes, tidal waves, earthquakes, thunderstorms, forest fires, you name it. When a scientist began to speculate that the age of dinosaurs ended when the earth was struck by an asteroid or comet, that really caught my attention. So did the eruption of Mount St. Helens. I only wish I could have seen it in person—from a safe distance, of course."[*]

[*] "Will Hobbs Talks about *Jackie's Wild Seattle*," *Will Hobbs Official Website*—Jackie's Wild Seattle *Idea Page*, www.willhobbsauthor.com/bookspages/book%20ideas%20pages/jackieswildseattle.html.

New Jersey. Cody has an excellent view of the lower Manhattan skyline. He arrives at the river's edge just as the second airliner crashes into the south tower of the World Trade Center. Shannon tells Uncle Neal:

> He saw the airplane coming, saw it hit the building, saw the ball of flame and everything. Everybody knew that the twin towers were gigantic office buildings with tens of thousands of people working inside. Mrs. Donnelly said everybody just stood there on the bluff, petrified. There was nothing to do but watch the tallest skyscrapers in New York City burn. Suddenly, from the top down, one of them just collapsed. They saw it fall, saw the dust clouds boil up and blot out lower Manhattan. Joey's mom said that people started crying, screaming. Cody and Joey were really, really scared.[99]

In the story, Cody's soccer coach, who worked in the twin towers, loses his life in the attack.

Readers of *Jackie's Wild Seattle* learn that because of the September 11 attacks, 7-year-old Cody Young has retreated into his own world. He displays a fascination for earthquakes, volcanoes, and other destructive forces of nature. The circle of healing that Shannon and Cody find at the wildlife center helps Cody emerge from his shell. He loses interest in natural disasters and becomes devoted to saving lives. The circle of healing also helps Shannon deal with her own fears. In the book, the children's parents are physicians who join Doctors Without Borders, the international aid agency. Shannon's parents are assigned to treat refugees who escaped the rule of the Taliban, the former governing body of Afghanistan that permitted the September 11 terrorists to train in their country. In fact, Shannon and Cody are sent to stay with their uncle because their parents are spending the summer working for Doctors Without Borders. Shannon spends much of the book worried about the safety of her parents because they are assigned to duty at refugee camps in Pakistan and Afghanistan, and are working very close to the war zone.

Hobbs notes that when he is imagining a story, he tries not to think in a straight line:

> I try to stay open to the possibilities, especially ones that will lend depth and complexity to the characters. I started writing this story only a couple of months after September 11. The emotional wounds all of us were feeling were still fresh. I remembered Kaye Baxter's phrase "the circle of healing" from my visits to Sarvey. I began to imagine a story in which that circle includes wildlife rescue and rehabilitation yet has a broader context. What if the girl telling the story, the girl and her little brother, lived very close to Manhattan? Maybe just across the Hudson River? What if the little brother was an eyewitness to the plane crashing into the Trade Center? Maybe their healing from the devastating effects of those events could happen far away, the following summer, when they were visiting their uncle in Seattle and helping sick and injured wildlife.[100]

One major difference between *Jackie's Wild Seattle* and Hobbs's other books is his decision to place the story in a city and its suburbs rather than the wilderness. Certainly, Hobbs gives his usual vivid descriptions of the countryside. From atop the Space Needle, the famous tall building that serves as Seattle's most familiar landmark, Shannon describes Cody's reaction to what she sees of the Washington countryside. She says:

> Forget about the stunning views of the downtown skyline, the neighborhoods and Lake Washington, the harbor and the

cruise ships, and the island-sprinkled waterways of Puget Sound leading out to the Pacific. Cody had eyes only for the gigantic glacier-covered mountain to the southeast. "Mount Rainier," he whispered reverently. "That mountain is one of the biggest disasters waiting to happen in the whole world. When it blows its top, it's going to be *major*."[101]

Hobbs does place the wildlife center about 50 miles north of the city. For the most part, though, the adventures of Uncle Neal, Shannon, and Cody take place along urban streets and suburban housing developments and shopping centers. Early in the book, Uncle Neal rescues a baby eagle that falls out of a nest after being startled by a car's backfire—hardly the type of problem that would confront Cloyd Atcitty in the Rocky Mountains. With *Jackie's Wild Seattle*, Hobbs says, it was time to place one of his stories in an environment more famil- iar to his readers. "That was a lot of the appeal," he says.

> I could set a story about wildness, and young people's concerns for wildlife, in the sort of location where many of my readers live. I've been visiting Washington State for many years. I have relatives there. I have gotten to know the Seattle area very well. With Seattle being on the inside waters of the Pacific yet close to so many amazing mountains, especially Mount Rainier, people there are known for their passion for the outdoors and for wildlife.[102]

As with *Downriver* and *River Thunder*, Hobbs decided to make the main character a teenage girl. The character of Jessie in the two earlier books turned out to be very popular among Hobbs's female readers. He knew he had to find new ways to make girls the main characters of his stories. Shannon proves in *Jackie's Wild Seattle* that she is as capable as any boy. In one scene, Shannon must climb down a cliff to rescue a baby seal. Shannon is an accomplished rock climber, but nothing in her experience prepared her for the climb back up the cliff.

> With every ounce of strength I had, I kept climbing. To make things worse, the weight of the seal kept shifting from side to side, and the sick baby kept whimpering. It was hard to bear, how much pain it was in . . . . I don't know what it was— adrenaline, I guess. My booster rockets kicked in. Finally, I lifted myself one last time and felt the grip of Neal's good hand like a skyhook. I was on top and so was the seal.[103]

Sadly, the circle of healing does not include the baby seal, which dies in the story. One animal that is healed is Liberty, the bald eagle saved by Uncle Neal. Again, the story of the eagle is drawn from the truth. In real life, the eagle was named Freedom. She was saved by a Sarvey Wildlife Center volunteer named Jeff Guidry. As in the book, volunteers at the shelter nursed the eagle back to health. Guidry and the others have dedicated themselves to saving the life of America's most treasured bird. Freedom is still unable to fly—the damage to her wings was too severe—but she serves as an ambassador for the Sarvey Wildlife Center. Kaye Baxter and Jeff Guidry visit many schools and other community organizations to talk about the work of the center and the importance of preserving wildlife. Usually, they take Freedom along to show young people what volunteers who devote themselves to a good cause can accomplish.

The character of Uncle Neal was also partly modeled on Jeff Guidry. In real life, Guidry survived his cancer, much as Uncle Neal survives the disease in *Jackie's Wild Seattle*. In both cases, saving the life of a baby eagle gave the two men the strength to fight the disease. Dianne Johnson, a Sarvey volunteer, says:

Freedom is alive because Jeff fought for her life, and there is no doubt Freedom sensed his love and commitment. Jeff gave Freedom the support she needed to want to live. . . . Only a short time ago, Jeff was informed there was no trace of the disease left in his body. He immediately left for the center. When he took Freedom out of her [pen], she did something she had never done before: She extended her wings and wrapped them around him. The circle of healing was now complete.[104]

Leaving Protection *is a mystery story that also examines the salmon fishing trade off the coast of Alaska. As part of his research for the book, Will Hobbs spent a week working on a fishing troller. He worked 15 hours a day.*

8

Adventures in the North

FOR MANY YEARS, archaeologists believed the first Americans arrived in Alaska some 14,000 years ago by walking across a land bridge that existed at the time, connecting Siberia, in Russia, with what would one day become the fiftieth state. The land bridge has since sunk into the ocean, leaving behind a narrow channel of sea known as the Bering Strait. In recent years, some archaeologists have challenged that assumption. They suggest the first Americans may have arrived as early as 30,000 years ago. These scientists believe the first Americans didn't walk over but made their way across the Pacific Ocean in boats, following the coastline from Asia to Alaska.

Hobbs explores these issues in his book *Wild Man Island*. It is a story of survival for 14-year-old Andy Galloway, who gets lost while kayaking along Alaska's coastline. A storm blows Andy's kayak ashore onto Alaska's rugged Admiralty Island. Andy encounters a hermit hunting with a spear. A friendly dog leads Andy into a cave where he finds Stone Age tools and weapons.

Hobbs had kayaked along the Alaska coast and was anxious to develop a story based on his adventures. When he learned that scientists had been making new discoveries about the arrival of the first Americans, Hobbs knew he'd found the perfect opportunity to write an adventure story wrapped around a true scientific mystery:

Several years went by after my sea kayaking trips with me not knowing if a story would grow out of those experiences or not. The kayaking, the natural history, and the place didn't seem like enough. I like to write stories that are "adventure plus." I try not to underestimate my readers. Kids appreciate learning new things as they're reading an exciting story. I could picture the adventure part, but the "plus" part was lacking. Then one day an article caught my eye about an alternate explanation of who the first Americans might have been. Fabulous new fossil discoveries were being made on Prince of Wales Island in southeast Alaska. It turns out a good portion of this island and others hadn't been under ice during the last Ice Age, as was previously thought. Animals living on ice-free islands in the northern Pacific could have provided a food source for seafaring people who came to North America by water, hugging the coastlines, before the land bridge opened up. I began to picture a kid shipwrecked in a kayak and winding up in a cave that might be hiding evidence of these earlier travelers.[105]

Hobbs has long been fascinated with the beauty of the wilderness north of the continental United States. Indeed, he has based five books on adventures in Alaska as well as the neighboring Canadian wilderness: *Wild Man Island*, *Far North, Jason's Gold* and its sequel *Down the Yukon*, and his latest book, *Leaving Protection*.

Although the stories are set in the same corner of the planet, they explore vastly different themes. While *Wild Man Island* examines a scientific question, *Far North* is a story of survival. Two boys, Gabe Rogers and Raymond Providence, fight the elements in *Far North*, which takes place in Canada's Northwest Territories, with the help of a Dene Indian elder named Johnny Raven. Hobbs says he hopes readers of *Far North* "suffer a good case of virtual frostbite turning the pages. At the end, I hope they'll say to themselves, 'What an amazing country that is, and what amazing people they must be who've known how to live in it for thousands of years.'"[106]

Leaving Protection examines the salmon fishing trade off the coast of Alaska and includes a mystery surrounding the valuable "possession plaques" left by early Russian explorers. *Jason's Gold* and *Down the Yukon* are stories set in the final years of the nineteenth century during the Klondike Gold Rush. In 1897 news of a gold strike in the Yukon Territory of Canada reached Seattle, triggering a stampede to the Klondike gold fields. Helping guide Jason Hawthorn is a young prospector named Jack London, who will in real life go on to become one of America's greatest novelists. Years before he wrote *The Call of the Wild*, *The Sea Wolf*, and *White Fang*, London attempted to make his fortune mining for gold in the Klondike. Bound for the Canadian goldfields, he traveled to Alaska in 1897 with his brother-in-law, Captain James H. Shepard. In *Jason's Gold*, Hobbs says, "I have endeavored to portray Jack London's history as accurately as possible, down to the scarlet long underwear he wore while toting his 150-pound loads up the Chilkoot Pass on a sweltering day in late August. Jack disposed of Captain Shepard's outfit after the older man turned back, for health reasons, before ascending the pass. It occurred to me that in my novel, Jack London could convey his brother-in-law's outfit to my protagonist, who would be in need of one."[107]

In *Jason's Gold*, Jason makes his way from New York to Seattle to catch up with his older brothers, who are heading for the Klondike. To get to Alaska, he stows away on a ship but is discovered by crewmen once the vessel reaches Juneau. Kicked off the ship and robbed and beaten by thugs, Jason wanders along a beach where he encounters Jack London making camp. London shows him kindness, giving Jason food and supplies, and helping him in his quest to find his brothers. Jason also finds romance when he meets a Canadian girl named Jamie Dunavant. Jamie and her father, Homer Dunavant, are also searching for gold in the Klondike. "We caught the Klondicitis bad, sold the farm, took the Canadian Pacific west to Vancouver and sailed there," Jamie tells Jason.[108]

In *Jason's Gold*, Homer Dunavant is a poet. Hobbs based the character of Jamie's father on another important literary figure of the Klondike—British-born poet Robert Service, who arrived on the heels of the gold rush and found fame celebrating it in poetry. He is the author of "The Cremation of Sam McGee," "The Shooting of Dan McGrew," and "The Spell of the Yukon," among other poems. "The Shooting of Dan McGrew" first appeared in a local newspaper in Whitehorse, a town in the Yukon Territory, where Service found a job as a bank teller.

In *Jason's Gold*, Jamie recites one of her father's poems to Jason.

Oh, they scratches the earth and it tumbles out,

More than your hands can hold.

For the hills above and plains beneath,

Are cracking and busting with gold.[109]

When Jamie asks, "How do you like it Jason?" Jason responds, "It makes me want to get up there and start digging."[110]

Did you know...

In *Jason's Gold*, Jason Hawthorn searches for his older brothers during the Klondike Gold Rush. As a boy, Will Hobbs says he always seemed to be following his older brothers, Greg and Ed, and that is why he dedicated the book to them, as well as to his younger brother, Joe.

"We've always been close, and I knew from the outset that making this a 'brothers story' would add layers of emotional reality for me," says Hobbs. "Like me, Jason has two older brothers. At the same time he is adamant about establishing his independence from them, he feels a very powerful connectedness to them. In my story, Jason is trying to catch up with his brothers, who've left Seattle for the Klondike three days before him. As a kid, I remember always hustling to catch up with my brothers, whether it was on the baseball field, in school, or learning to ice skate while we were living up in Alaska."*

Hobbs's brother Greg went on to practice law and serves as a justice on the Colorado Supreme Court. Ed Hobbs spent a career as a physician in the Air Force, and then retired to open a private practice in San Antonio. Joe Hobbs is a professor of geography at the University of Missouri and has written a book about the geography and people of the Middle East. Hobbs's sister, Barbara, is a home health-care nurse in California.

* "Will Hobbs Talks about *Jason's Gold* and *Down the Yukon*," Will Hobbs Official Website—Jason's Gold *and* Down the Yukon *Idea Page,* www.willhobbsauthor.com/bookspages/book%20ideas%20pages/jasonyukon.html

In *Down the Yukon*, Jason and Jamie return for another adventure. This time, the two young people enter a canoe race down the Yukon River from Dawson City to Nome. They hope to win the prize of $20,000, which Jason needs to buy back his family's sawmill. Although the race is fictional, it stems from an actual event that occurred in 1899. Hobbs says:

> I knew that the news of a big gold strike at Cape Nome, out on the Bering Sea, electrified Dawson City that summer. Thousands and thousands of people left town. They floated fifteen hundred miles down the Yukon River and then crossed Norton Sound to reach the new gold mecca of Nome. Now I could jump into the history of the new gold rush as well as researching the course of the Yukon River across Alaska. As you know, I love to write stories that involve a journey, and this would be a marvelous journey for Jason and Jamie to make together.[111]

As a young boy, Hobbs had lived in Alaska. As an adult, he traveled through the state's breathtaking landscape. He brought all he knew about Alaska to *Jason's Gold* and *Down the Yukon*.

> A lifetime of backpacking—carrying heavy loads over mountain passes—helped me to describe Jason's struggles on the Chilkoot Pass. My canoeing and rafting experiences, including those in Canada's Yukon and Northwest Territories, came in handy as I described Jason's journey by canoe down the upper Yukon River. My winter camping experiences at twenty degrees below zero at high altitude in Colorado helped me to write the winter scenes.[112]

Hobbs had extensive experience kayaking along rough coastlines, canoeing down swift rivers, and backpacking through rugged mountains; however, none of those experiences prepared him for the adventure he would live while researching *Leaving Protection*. The book, which was published in 2004, tells the story of 16-year-old Robbie Daniels, who longs to find a job on a king salmon fishing boat. Unexpectedly, Robbie lands a job aboard the *Storm Petrel*, a salmon troller captained by Tor Torsen, a legendary fisherman. The story takes place off Prince of Wales Island near Alaska's southern coast. Since much of the story unfolds aboard Torsen's troller, Hobbs felt there was only one way to truly talk about the life of king salmon fishermen. He had to spend time aboard a salmon troller, doing the work he planned to have Robbie do. According to Hobbs:

> On a number of previous trips to southeast Alaska, I'd fallen in love with the picturesque salmon trollers, and always imagined what it would be like to work on one. When a teacher on Prince of Wales Island, Julie Yates, invited me to work with her and her father on his troller, I jumped at the chance. George Yates is in his fourth decade of trolling, and I was lucky enough to get in on his most productive king salmon season in years.[113]

And so for a week, Hobbs labored aboard George Yates's fishing troller. He worked 15 hours a day. "My job was to clean and ice the fish, and I really got worked. It was a great feeling. I've done a quite a bit of physical labor in my life—building houses, stuff like that—but the only thing to compare with this was six weeks I spent picking fruit in Idaho when I first got out of college."[114] Here is how Hobbs describes the work, as Robbie performed it:

> The rinse bin on each side refreshed, I climbed down into the fish hold and began the stoop work I was hired for. I was set to begin stowing our treasure. Troll-caught are the finest restaurant-quality wild salmon, the most expensive on account of being the most labor-intensive—cleaned and bled within minutes of being caught, iced a few degrees above freezing, then rushed to market by jet.

I began by bedding the forward right section of the hold with a few inches of ice. Then I returned to the central floor where I'd thrown the salmon. I lifted that fifty-pounder with both arms, duck-walked it forward, used the aluminum scoop to fill its body and gill cavity with ice, then laid it gently off to the right. Extra-large were paying $1.21 a pound. I was looking at a sixty-dollar fish. My share . . . nine dollars. Not bad!

My back was already fit to breaking. Hours of bending over the stern to gaff the fish, bending over the cleaning bin, and stooping in the hold were taking their toll. It felt like the fish knife was planted deep between my shoulder blades.[115]

Of course, the novel is about a lot more than just salmon fishing. As Hobbs says, he always looks to write a book that is "adventure plus." In this case, Robbie discovers that Torsen is in possession of a centuries-old journal and is searching for the priceless possession plaques buried by early Russian explorers along the Alaska coast. The journal was written by Nikolai Rezanov, a Russian aristocrat who hoped to claim more of the Northwest for Russia. In 1799, Rezanov established the Russian America Company, which established a fur-trading settlement at Sitka along Alaska's southern coastline. Russia owned Alaska until it sold the territory to the United States in 1867.

Hobbs and his wife Jean visited Sitka in 2002 and, while touring a museum, saw a facsimile of the only possession plaque ever discovered. Historical records indicate that there were 20 in all, buried along the coasts of Alaska and perhaps farther south. The missing plaques would be priceless if discovered. "I had that to draw on when I needed that missing element that would make the story go," Hobbs says of the plaques. "For years, I had been reading about the history of the Russians in Alaska, so I had quite a bit to draw on that

Will Hobbs kayaked along the Alaskan coast and wanted to develop a story based on this adventure. The result was Wild Man Island, *an adventure story about the first Stone Age visitors to America who crossed over from Siberia.*

I was already familiar with. [116] Rezanov's journal is a fictional device. It's a virtual treasure map, and *Leaving Protection* is something of a treasure story." [117]

In *Leaving Protection*, Robbie learns of Torsen's scheme to sell the plaques to collectors, reaping perhaps millions of dollars. As with most Hobbs adventures, the characters must also fight against nature, facing huge waves and savage storms. *Leaving Protection* includes all the elements that Hobbs has been including in his stories since he first wrote *Pride of the West* a quarter-century ago. His readers have come to count on Hobbs to tell them a good story, give them a history lesson, and help them appreciate the beauty of the wilderness that remains a part of the North American landscape. As Hobbs says, "My first hope for my novels is that they will tell a good story, that the reader will keep turning the pages and will hate to see the story end. Beyond that, I hope to be inspiring a love for the natural world. I'd like my readers to appreciate and care more about what's happening to wild creatures, wild places, and the diversity of life." [117]

1 Will Hobbs, *Changes in Latitudes* (New York: Avon Books, 1988), 36.

2 Quoted in Scot Peacock, ed. "Will Hobbs," *Something About the Author*, vol. 127 (Farmington Hills, MI: Gale Group, 2002), 79.

3 Hobbs, *Changes in Latitudes*, 65.

4 "Will Hobbs Talks about *Changes in Latitude*," *Will Hobbs Official Website*—Changes in Latitudes *Idea Page*, www.willhobbsauthor.com/bookspages/book%20ideas%20pages/changeslatit.html.

5 Ibid.

6 Hobbs, *Changes in Latitudes*, 162.

7 Quoted in Scot Peacock, ed. "Will Hobbs," *Contemporary Authors: New Revision Series*, vol. 124 (Farmington Hills, MI: Gale Thomson, 2004), 257.

8 "Will Hobbs Talks about *Changes in Latitude*," *Will Hobbs Official Website*—Changes in Latitudes *Idea Page*.

9 Quoted in Scot Peacock, ed. "Will Hobbs," *Something About the Author*, vol. 127, 80.

10 Ibid.

11 Ibid.

12 Ibid.

13 Ibid., 81.

14 Ibid., 82.

15 Ibid.

16 Ibid., 84.

17 Ibid.

18 Ibid., 85.

19 Ibid., 86.

20 Ibid.

21 Ibid.

22 Ibid., 88.

23 Ibid.

24 Ibid., 89.

25 Ibid., 90.

26 Quoted in Diane Telgen, ed. "Will Hobbs," *Something About the Author*, vol. 72 (Detroit, MI: Gale Research, 1993), 111.

27 Ibid.

28 Quoted in Scot Peacock, ed. "Will Hobbs," *Something About the Author*, vol. 127, 90.

29 Will Hobbs, *Bearstone* (New York: Simon and Schuster, 1989), 65.

30 Hal Marcovitz's interview with Will Hobbs, November 22, 2004.

31 Hobbs, *Bearstone*, 15.

32 Ibid., 16.

33 Ibid., 149.

34 "Will Hobbs Talks about *Bearstone* and *Beardance*," *Will Hobbs Official Website*—Bearstone *and* Beardance *Idea Page*, www.willhobbsauthor.com/bookspages/book%20ideas%20pages/bearstondanc.html.

35 Hobbs, *Bearstone*, 106–107.

36 Ibid., 82.

37 Hal Marcovitz's interview with Will Hobbs, November 22, 2004.

38 Ibid.

39 "Will Hobbs Talks about *Bearstone* and *Beardance*," *Will Hobbs Official Website*—Bearstone *and* Beardance *Idea Page*.

40 Ibid.

41 Ibid.

42 Quoted in W.L. Rusho, *Everett Ruess: A Vagabond for Beauty* (Salt Lake City, UT: Peregrine Smith Books, 1983), 158.

43 Ibid., x.

44 "Will Hobbs Talks about *The Big Wander*," *Will Hobbs Official Website*—The Big Wander *Idea Page, www.willhobbsauthor.com/ bookspages/book%20ideas%20pa ges/bigwander.html*.

45 Ibid.

46 Quoted in Edgar H. Thompson, "An Interview with Will Hobbs: How His Novels Come Into Being," *Alan Review* 22, no. 1 (1994), 7–10.

47 Ibid.

48 Ibid.

49 Ibid.

50 Ibid.

51 Will Hobbs, *The Big Wander* (New York: Macmillan Publishing Company, 1992), 118–119.

52 Will Hobbs, "Untangling the Lines: Revision," *Writing!* (October 2003), 5.

53 Ibid.

54 Ibid.

55 *Will Hobbs Official Website— About Writing, www.willhobb sauthor.com/writing.html*.

56 Quoted in Scot Peacock, ed. "Will Hobbs," *Something About the Author*, vol. 127, 78.

57 *Will Hobbs Official Website— About Writing, www.willhobb sauthor.com/writing.html*.

58 Quoted in Alan Hedblad, ed. "Will Hobbs," *Something About the Author*, vol. 110 (Farmington Hills, MI: Gale Thomson, 2000), 110.

59 *Will Hobbs Official Website— About Writing, www.willhobb sauthor.com/writing.html*.

60 Ibid.

61 Will Hobbs, *Downriver* (New York: Simon and Schuster, 1991), 7–8.

62 "Will Hobbs Talks about *Downriver* and *River Thunder*," *Will Hobbs Official Website—* Downriver *and* River Thunder *Idea Page, www.willhobbsauthor .com/bookspages/book%20ideas %20pages/downrrthun.html*.

63 Amy Benfer, "Girl Revisited," *The New York Times* (March 6, 2004).

64 Quoted in Bobbie Ann Mason, *The Girl Sleuth: On the Trail of Nancy Drew, Judy Bolton and Cherry Ames* (Athens, GA: University of Georgia Press, 1995), 53.

65 Ibid.

66 Hal Marcovitz's interview with Will Hobbs, November 22, 2004.

67 Hobbs, *Downriver*, 74.

68 Ibid., 192.

69 Ibid., 195.

70 Hal Marcovitz's interview with Will Hobbs, November 22, 2004.

71 "Will Hobbs Talks about *Downriver* and *River Thunder*," *Will Hobbs Official Website—* Downriver *and* River Thunder *Idea Page.*

72 Will Hobbs, *River Thunder* (New York: Delacorte Press, 1997), 201.

73 John Wesley Powell, *Down the Colorado* (New York: Arrowhead Press, 1988), 43–44.

74 Hobbs, *Downriver*, 69.

75 Hobbs, *River Thunder*, 200–201.

76 "Will Hobbs Talks about *Downriver* and *River Thunder*," *Will Hobbs Official Website—*Downriver *and* River Thunder *Idea Page*.

77 Ibid.

78 "Will Hobbs Talks about *Kokopelli's Flute*," *Will Hobbs Official Website—*Kokopelli's Flute *Idea Page*, *www.willhobbsauthor.com/bookspages/book%20ideas%20pages/kokopelli.html*.

79 Will Hobbs, *Kokopelli's Flute* (New York: Simon and Schuster, 1995), 18.

80 Hal Marcovitz's interview with Will Hobbs, November 22, 2004.

81 Ibid.

82 "Will Hobbs Talks about *Kokopelli's Flute*," *Will Hobbs Official Website—*Kokopelli's Flute *Idea Page*.

83 Hobbs, *Kokopelli's Flute*, 25.

84 "Will Hobbs Talks about *Kokopelli's Flute*," *Will Hobbs Official Website—*Kokopelli's Flute *Idea Page*.

85 Ibid.

86 Ibid.

87 Will Hobbs, *Ghost Canoe* (New York: William Morrow and Co., 1997), 195.

88 Quoted in Edgar H. Thompson, "An Interview with Will Hobbs," *Alan Review* 27, no. 2 (Winter 2000), 5–6.

89 Will Hobbs, *Jackie's Wild Seattle* (New York: HarperCollins, 2003), 175.

90 Ibid., 171.

91 "Will Hobbs Talks about *Jackie's Wild Seattle*," *Will Hobbs Official Website—*Jackie's Wild Seattle *Idea Page*, *www.willhobbsauthor.com/bookspages/book%20ideas%20pages/jackieswildseattle.html*.

92 Hal Marcovitz's interview with Will Hobbs, November 22, 2004.

93 Ibid.

94 Ibid.

95 Hobbs, *Jackie's Wild Seattle*, 164.

96 Ibid.

97 "Will Hobbs Talks about *Jackie's Wild Seattle*," *Will Hobbs Official Website—*Jackie's Wild Seattle *Idea Page*.

98 Quoted in Charlie Langdon, "Hobbs' Book Tells of Kids and 9-11," *Durango Herald* (April 20, 2003).

99 Hobbs, *Jackie's Wild Seattle*, 17.

100 "Will Hobbs Talks about *Jackie's Wild Seattle*," *Will Hobbs Official Website—*Jackie's Wild Seattle *Idea Page*.

101 Hobbs, *Jackie's Wild Seattle*, 16.

102 "Will Hobbs Talks about *Jackie's Wild Seattle*," *Will Hobbs Official Website—*Jackie's Wild Seattle *Idea Page*.

103 Hobbs, *Jackie's Wild Seattle*, 119–120.

104 Jeff Guidry, "The Circle of Healing," Sarvey Wildlife Center website, *www.sarveywildlife.org/Story.aspx?id=7.*

105 Quoted in James Blasingame, "Wild Man Island," *Journal of Adolescent and Adult Literacy* 26, no. 5 (February 1, 2003), 442.

106 "Will Hobbs Talks about *Far North,*" *Will Hobbs Official Website*—Far North *Idea Page, www.willhobbsauthor.com/bookspages/book%20ideas%20pages/farnorth.html.*

107 Will Hobbs, *Jason's Gold* (New York: William Morrow and Co., 1999), 219.

108 Ibid., 70.

109 Ibid., 71.

110 Ibid.

111 "Will Hobbs Talks about *Jason's Gold* and *Down the Yukon,*" *Will Hobbs Official Website*—Jason's Gold *and* Down the Yukon *Idea Page, www.willhobbsauthor.com/bookspages/book%20ideas%20pages/jasonyukon.html.*

112 Ibid.

113 Ibid.

114 Ibid.

115 Will Hobbs, *Leaving Protection* (New York: HarperCollins, 2004), 42–43.

116 "Will Hobbs Talks about *Leaving Protection,*" *Will Hobbs Official Website*—Leaving Protection *Idea Page,* www.willhobsauthor.com/bookspages/book%20ideas%20pages/protection.html.

117 Hal Marcovitz's interview with Will Hobbs, November 22, 2004

118 "Will Hobbs Talks about *Leaving Protection,*" *Will Hobbs Official Website*—Leaving Protection *Idea Page.*

1947 August 22, Will Hobbs born in Pittsburgh, Pennsylvania.

1948 Moves to the Panama Canal Zone with family.

1951 Moves to Falls Church, Virginia, with family and rescues box turtles from abuse by neighborhood children.

1955 Family settles in Anchorage, Alaska, where Hobbs hears the story *Call It Courage* read in class.

1957 Moves to Marin County, California, with family.

1961 Moves to Texas with family; enrolls in Central Catholic High School in San Antonio, Texas; starts developing his talent for writing.

1964 Moves back to Marin County for senior year in high school.

1965 Enrolls at Notre Dame University in Indiana.

1963 Transfers to Stanford University after freshman year at Notre Dame University; majors in English.

1969 Graduates from Stanford. Enrolls in graduate school but leaves before completing doctoral degree with a master's degree. Moves in with friends, writes poetry, and finds a job picking grapes in the Anderson Valley.

1971 Teaches school in Upper Lake, California.

1972 Moves to New Mexico, marries Jean Loftus on December 20. Earns teaching certificate at New Mexico Highland University.

1973 Moves to Pagosa Springs in southwest Colorado; teaches at Pagosa Springs High School and Junior High School.

1977 Enrolls in the graduate school of the University of Oregon; studies literature of the American West and teaches freshman composition.

1978 Returns to Colorado and builds a home near Durango; teaches at Miller Junior High School.

1979 Rows his first white water river.

1980 Writes an unpublished novel titled *Pride of the West*.

1983 Rafts through the Grand Canyon for the first time.

1988 His first novel, *Changes in Latitudes*, published.

1989 *Bearstone*, a rewritten version of *Pride of the West*, published.

1990 Resigns from teaching job and devotes himself full time to writing.

1991 *Downriver* published.

1992 *The Big Wander* published.

1993 *Beardance*, a sequel to *Bearstone*, published.

1995 *Kokopelli's Flute* published.

1996 *Far North* published.

1997 *Beardream*, a picture book for young readers, published. Also published is *River Thunder*, a sequel to *Downriver*, and *Ghost Canoe*.

1998 Picture book, *Howling Hill*, and *The Maze* published.

1999 *Jason's Gold* published.

2001 *Down the Yukon*, a sequel to *Jason's Gold,* published.

2002 *Wild Man Island* published.

2003 *Jackie's Wild Seattle* published.

2004 *Leaving Protection* published.

BEARSTONE

Cloyd Atcitty is a troubled Ute Indian boy who spends a summer helping an old farmer, Walter Landis, who has recently lost his wife. Cloyd and Walter form a bond. Walter helps Cloyd grow up, while Cloyd provides Walter with the inspiration to keep farming and reopen his old gold mine, which he hasn't visited in 40 years. Along the way, Cloyd explores the land of his ancestors and tries to save Colorado's last grizzly bear.

BEARDANCE

In the sequel to *Bearstone*, Cloyd Atcitty and Walter Landis return to the mountains in search of a lost Spanish gold mine. Cloyd learns of the existence of another grizzly bear and risks his life to protect the bear's cubs.

THE BIG WANDER

Inspired by the life of poet and artist Everett Ruess, the story follows 14-year-old Clay Lancaster as he travels from Monument Valley to rugged Glen Canyon in Utah in search of his lost uncle, a former rodeo star. Clay finds romance and learns that his uncle is trying to save the area's last wild horses.

CHANGES IN LATITUDES

Travis and Teddy are on a family vacation in Mexico when they find themselves caught up in an adventure to save the lives of olive ridley sea turtles, which are being driven to the brink of extinction, killed for their meat, shells, and eggs.

DOWNRIVER

Seven troubled young people steal a van and sneak away from their counselor to go on a white-water rafting adventure on the Colorado River. The story is narrated by Jessie, Hobbs's first female protagonist, who at the beginning of the adventure is very much a follower. When a scorpion stings one of the teenagers, Jessie takes charge and leads everyone to safety.

RIVER THUNDER

Jessie and her companions from *Downriver* return for another white-water adventure in the Grand Canyon. This time, they are a bit more mature, but old rivalries soon emerge, and Jessie must again rise to the challenge as the group faces unprecedented high water on the Colorado River.

JASON'S GOLD

Jason Hawthorn heads for the Klondike to join his brothers in searching for gold. On the way, he must endure the rigors of the Dead Horse Trail, the Chilkoot Pass, and a 500-mile trip by canoe down the Yukon River. Aided by a young prospector named Jack London, Jason and his dog face moose, bears, and a Yukon winter in this story of survival.

DOWN THE YUKON

A sequel to *Jason's Gold*, Jason Hawthorn's new adventure takes him on a canoe race to Nome for a $20,000 prize, which Jason hopes to use to buy back his family's sawmill. Jason and the girl he loves, Jamie Dunavant, share the canoe in a race across Alaska and face the hazards of the Yukon River and the open sea.

FAR NORTH

A seaplane floats over a waterfall and leaves 14-year-old Gabe Rogers and his friend, Raymond Providence, a Dene Indian, stranded near the Nahanni River in Canada's Northwest Territories. Gabe and Raymond spend the winter along the Nahanni, where they are helped by Johnny Raven, a Dene elder, who shows them how to hunt beavers, trap rabbits, and make snowshoes and mittens out of animal hides. When Raven dies, the two boys find themselves surviving on their own.

GHOST CANOE

Set in 1874 on Cape Flattery in Washington State, *Ghost Canoe* follows Nathan MacAllister, the 14-year-old son of a lighthouse keeper, as he finds clues that will solve the murder of the captain of a doomed sailing ship. Meanwhile, Nathan learns to hunt, fish, and survive the treachery of the murderer under the guidance of his friend, Lighthouse George, a member of the Makah whaling tribe.

JACKIE'S WILD SEATTLE

In the summer of 2002, Shannon and Cody are sent to Seattle, Washington, to live with their Uncle Neal, because their parents are in Pakistan providing medical care to Afghan refugees. They discover their uncle is a volunteer for a wildlife rescue organization. When their uncle gets injured, Shannon and Cody serve as his hands, rescuing a baby seal, a trapped coyote, and a lost and hungry bobcat.

KOKOPELLI'S FLUTE

The story follows Tepary Jones as he makes the mistake of playing a few notes on an ancient, magical flute during an eclipse of the moon. By day, he inhabits his own body, by night, he becomes a pack rat. Tep must use his new powers to track down the looters of an ancient cliff dwelling and find medicinal herbs to save his mother's life.

LEAVING PROTECTION

Robbie Daniels lands a job on a salmon boat captained by the legendary fisherman Tor Torsen. Fishing near Prince of Wales Island in Alaska, Robbie is living his dream until he discovers Torsen's true intentions—to find and sell the valuable possession plaques left behind by early Russian explorers laying claim to Alaska.

THE MAZE

The plight of the California condors is told in the story, which finds young Rick Walter stranded in the Maze, a remote region of Canyonlands National Park in Utah. Stumbling into the camp of biologist Lon Peregrino, Rick discovers Lon's mission to release the endangered birds back into the wild. He also discovers how to fly like a bird on the wings of a hang glider.

WILD MAN ISLAND

While on a sea kayaking trip in Alaska, Andy Galloway explores the site where his archaeologist father died searching for evidence of the first Americans. Soon, a storm sweeps Andy's kayak far across the strait, where he swims to Admiralty Island, an immense wilderness of forests, rain, and bears. Andy's tale of survival leads him to the cave of the "Wild Man," who may provide the boy with a link to the truth sought by his father.

1991 *Bearstone*

1993 *Beardance, Changes in Latitudes*

1994 *The Big Wander*

1995 *Downriver*

1996 *Far North*

1997 *River Thunder, Kokopelli's Flute, Ghost Canoe*

1998 *Howling Hill*

1999 *The Maze*

2000 *Jason's Gold, Down the Yukon, Beardream*

2003 *Wild Man, Jackie's Wild Seattle*

2004 *Leaving Protection*

ANDY GALLOWAY

In *Wild Man Island*, Andy Galloway searches for clues that will lead him to the discovery his father died trying to find. His trail leads him into the caves of Alaska's remote Admiralty Island, where he finds evidence of ancient travelers to America.

CLAY LANCASTER

Clay Lancaster, the main character in *The Big Wander*, is inspired by Everett Ruess, a young artist who roamed the rugged wilderness of the American southwest in search of beauty. The story is centered in the Glen Canyon area of Utah, which is where Ruess was last seen alive. Lancaster, 14, searches for a lost uncle, an old rodeo star. Along the way he finds romance and also learns about the plight of wild horses, which his uncle is trying to save.

CLOYD ATCITTY

Cloyd Atcitty, a Ute Indian who comes of age in *Bearstone*, lives in a group home until he spends the summer with an old rancher named Walter. On a trip into the mountains, Cloyd bonds with the spirit of his people and the brotherhood they share with bears, and rescues Walter from a mining accident. Walter becomes the first father figure in Cloyd's life. Cloyd's adventures continue in *Beardance*, in which he protects two grizzly bear cubs.

GABE ROGERS AND RAYMOND PROVIDENCE

Gabe Rogers and Raymond Providence survive the loss of a float plane over the falls in *Far North*, but must spend the winter in Canada's remote Northwest Territories. They are helped by a Dene Indian named Johnny Raven, who shows them the ways of winter survival.

JASON HAWTHORN

In *Jason's Gold*, Jason Hawthorn makes his way across country, then stows away on a ship bound for Alaska, where he will search for his brothers, meet author Jack London, find romance with Jamie Dunavant, and join the Klondike Gold Rush. In the book's sequel, *Down the Yukon*, Jason and Jamie enter a canoe race on the Yukon River in the rush to the new gold fields at Nome.

JESSIE

The central character of *Downriver* and *River Thunder*, Jessie faces the dangers of white-water rafting down the Colorado River. The two books follow her personal journey as well, as she overcomes her rebelliousness, rekindles her love of wild places, and finds her way home.

NATHAN MACALLISTER

In *Ghost Canoe*, 14-year-old Nathan MacAllister is the son of a lighthouse keeper. He befriends a Makah Indian named Lighthouse George, learns the ways of the Makah Indians, and unravels the murder of a sea captain by a conniving treasure-seeker.

RICK WALKER

Rick Walker is a troubled young man who has spent his life in foster homes and dead ends. In *The Maze*, Rick wanders into the stark and rugged region of Canyonlands National Park in Utah known as the Maze, where he discovers, through hang gliding, the ability to soar above his problems. He also learns about the plight of California condors, an endangered species of birds.

ROBBIE MCDANIEL

In *Leaving Protection*, 16-year-old Robbie McDaniel finds a job working for legendary salmon boat skipper Tor Torsen, then discovers Torsen has a far darker purpose for sailing the Alaskan coastal waters: to unearth and sell the priceless possession plaques buried two centuries ago by early Russian explorers.

SHANNON YOUNG

Shannon Young, the main character in *Jackie's Wild Seattle*, keeps an eye on her little brother Cody. She also helps troubled teenager Tyler break away from his abusive and alcoholic father and provides a shoulder for Uncle Neal to lean on. Shannon provides more than just emotional support, however, when she saves a baby seal by climbing down the face of a cliff and when she rescues a lost coyote from an elevator car.

TEPARY JONES

Tepary Jones is a young seed farmer who turns into a pack rat by night in Hobbs's story, *Kokopelli's Flute*. Only Tep's dog recognizes Tep in his pack rat form. Tep uses his power to thwart thieves who rob Anasazi Indian artifacts and to find herbs that will cure his mother of the hantavirus disease.

TRAVIS

Travis, the 16-year-old main character of *Changes in Latitudes*, is selfish and self-centered, but wakes up to the problems of others when he finds himself swimming with sea turtles and realizes just how much peril they face at the hands of poachers. Along with his brother Teddy, Travis gets caught up in the efforts of environmentalists to rescue the turtles.

1988 *Changes in Latitudes*, awarded Notable Children's Trade Book in the Field of Social Studies by the National Council for Social Studies and Children's Book Council. Winner of the Colorado Blue Spruce Award.

1989 *Bearstone*, awarded prize for Best Books for Young Adults, American Library Association and Teachers' Choices Award of the International Reading Association; selected for the Notable Children's Trade Book in the Field of Social Studies by the Council for Social Studies and Children's Book Council.

1991 *Downriver*, awarded by the American Library Association: Best Books for Young Adults, 100 Best of the Best Young Adult Books of the Past 25 years, 100 Best of the Best Young Adult Books of the Twentieth Century, and a Quick Pick for Reluctant Young Adult Readers. Also named to the Pick of the Lists, American Booksellers Association, and selected as a Book for the Teen Age, New York Public Library. Winner of the California Young Reader Medal and the Colorado Blue Spruce Award.

1992 *The Big Wander*, named a Best Book for Young Adults by the American Library Association and selected as a Book for the Teen Age by the New York Public Library.

1993 *Beardance*, named a Best Book for Young Adults by the American Library Association and selected as a Pick of the Lists by the American Booksellers Association.

1995 *Kokopelli's Flute*, named a Notable Children's Trade Book in the Field of Social Studies by the Council for Social Studies and Children's Book Council.

1996 *Far North*, awarded by the American Library Association: Best Books for Young Adults, Top Ten Young Adult Books for 1996, 100 Best of the Best Young Adult Books of the Twentieth Century, and a Quick Pick for Reluctant Young Adult Readers. Selected by the National Council for Social Studies and Children's Book Council as a Notable Children's Trade Book in the Field of Social Studies. Selected as a Young Adult Choice by the International Reading Association and a Book for the Teen Age by the New York Public Library. Selected as a Books in the Middle Outstanding Title by the Voice of Youth Advocates.

1997 *Ghost Canoe*, winner of the Edgar Allan Poe Award, Best Young Adult Mystery, awarded by the Mystery Writers of America. Also named Pick of the Lists by the American Booksellers Association and selected as a Book for the Teen Age by the New York Public

Library. Selected as a Book in the Middle Outstanding Title by the Voice of Youth Advocates. Winner of New Mexico's Land of Enchantment Award.

River Thunder, selected as a Young Adult Choice by the International Reading Association, named a selection of the Junior Library Guild, and picked as a Book for the Teen Age by the New York Public Library.

1998 *The Maze*, awarded by the American Library Association: Best Book for Young Adults, Popular Paperback for Young Adults, and a Quick Pick for Reluctant Young Adult Readers. Also named a Pick of the Lists by the American Booksellers Association and selected by the International Reading Association and Children's Book Council as a Teacher's Choice and Young Adult Choice.

1999 *Jason's Gold*, selected as a Best Book for Young Adults and named a Quick Pick for Reluctant Young Adult Readers, both by the American Library Association; selected as a Pick of the Lists by the American Booksellers Association and named Notable Children's Trade Book in the Field of Social Studies by the Council for Social Studies and Children's Book Council. Also selected as a Book for the Teen Age by the New York Public Library and picked as a Books in the Middle Outstanding Title by the Voice of Youth Advocates.

2001 *Down the Yukon*, selected a Book for the Teen Age by the New York Public Library.

2002 *Wild Man Island*, selected as an Outstanding Science Trade Book for Children by the National Science Teachers Association and the Children's Book Council. Also named a Book for the Teen Age by the New York Public Library.

2003 *Jackie's Wild Seattle*, selected by the New York Public Library as a Book for the Teen Age and named an Outstanding Science Trade Book for Children by the National Science Teachers Association and the Children's Book Council.

Will Hobbs is also the winner of several lifetime achievement awards. His novels have been nominated for state awards in more than 30 states.

Barber, Mike. "Basket Weaver's Legacy is Woven into Fabric of the Makah." *Seattle Post-Intelligencer*, August 22, 2002.

Benfer, Amy. "Girl Revisited." *New York Times*, March 6, 2004.

Blasingame, James. "Wild Man Island," *Journal of Adolescent and Adult Literacy* 46, no. 5 (February 1, 2003) 442.

"Favorite Questions about Will," Will Hobbs Official Website, *www.willhobbsauthor.com/questions.html*.

Hedblad, Alan, ed. *Something About the Author*. Vol. 110. Farmington Hills, MI: Gale Group, 2000.

Hobbs, Will. "Untangling the Lines: Revision." *Writing!*, October 2003.

"Just for Fun!" Will Hobbs Official Website, *www.willhobbsauthor.com/forfun.html*.

Langdon, Charlie. "Hobbs' Book Tells of Kids and 9-11." *Durango Herald*, April 20, 2003.

Mason, Bobbie Ann. *The Girl Sleuth: On the Trail of Nancy Drew, Judy Bolton and Cherry Ames*. Athens, GA: University of Georgia Press, 1995.

Parfit, Michael. "Dawn of Humans: Hunt for the First Americans." *National Geographic* 198, no. 6 (December 2000), 40–67.

Peacock, Scot, ed. *Contemporary Authors: New Revision Series* Vol. 124. Farmington Hills, MI: Thomson Gale, 2004.

Peacock, Scot, ed. *Something About the Author*. Vol. 127. Farmington Hills, MI: Gale Group, 2002.

Powell, John Wesley. *Down the Colorado: Diary of the First Trip Through the Grand Canyon*. New York: Arrowood Press, 1988.

Reiman, Mark. "Kaye Baxter: A Wild Animal's Best Friend." *Incredible People Magazine* 5, no. 37 (June 21, 2000).

Rusho, W.L. *Everett Ruess: A Vagabond for Beauty*. Salt Lake City, UT: Peregrine Smith Books, 1983.

Sperry, Armstrong. *Call It Courage*. New York: MacMillan Publishing Co., 1968.

Telgen, Diane, ed. *Something About the Author*. Vol. 72. Detroit, MI: Gale Research Inc, 1993.

Thompson, Edgar H. "An Interview with Will Hobbs: How His Novels Come Into Being." *Alan Review* 22, no. 1 (Fall 1994).

Thompson, Edgar H. "An Interview with Will Hobbs." *Alan Review* 27, no. 2 (Winter 2000).

Lourie, Peter. *Yukon River*. Honesdale, PA: Boyds Mills Press, 2000.

Marsh, Charles. *People of the Shining Mountains: The Utes of Colorado*. Boulder, CO: Pruett Publishing Company, 1982.

Pettit, Jan. *Utes, The Mountain People*. Boulder, CO: Johnson Books, 1990.

Stewart, Hilary. *Cedar: Tree of Life to the Northwest Indians*. Seattle, WA: University of Washington Press, 1995.

www.willhobbsauthor.com
[Will Hobbs's official website features summaries of his books, interviews with Hobbs for each of his books, and information for teachers on projects that use his books as guides.]

www.durango.org
[Will Hobbs's hometown of Durango, Colorado's website.]

www.hsus.org
[The Humane Society of the United States website provides the student with information on the plight of sea turtles and other endangered species.]

http://mountain-prairie.fws.gov/species/mammals/grizzly/
[U.S. Fish and Wildlife Service's Grizzly Bear Recovery website covers efforts made by the federal government to ensure the survival of the grizzly bears.]

www.powellmuseum.org
[The John Wesley Powell Memorial Museum in Page, Arizona, provides an abundant amount of information on the explorer who first rafted through the Grand Canyon.]

www.cdc.gov/ncidod/diseases/hanta/hps/index.htm
[U.S. Centers for Disease Control and Prevention's All About Hantaviruses web page.]

www.makah.com
[The Makah Cultural and Research Center maintains this official website of the Makah tribe.]

www.sarveywildlife.org
[The website for the Sarvey Wildlife Center in Arlington, Washington.]

All photos generously provided by Jean and Will Hobbs.

HAL MARCOVITZ is a journalist who lives in Pennsylvania with his wife Gail and daughters Ashley and Michelle. He is the author of the satirical novel *Painting the White House* as well as more than 60 nonfiction books for young readers. His other titles in the WHO WROTE THAT? series include biographies of writers Bruce Coville and R.L. Stine.